DEADLY
INDIAN
SUMMER

DEADLY
INDIAN
SUMMER

A NOVEL BY

LEONARD SCHONBERG

SANTA FE
New Mexico

*THE EVENTS, PEOPLE, AND INCIDENTS IN THIS STORY
are the sole product of the author's imagination. The story is
fictional and any resemblance to individuals living or dead
is purely coincidental.*

Creation Myth (p.66) from *The Story of the American Indian*
by Paul Radin, Liveright Publishing Corp., New York.

House made of Dawn prayer (p.69) from Robert Northshield,
NBC News.

Sunstone books may be purchased for educational, business, or sales promotional use. For
information please write: Special Markets Department, Sunstone Press, P.O. Box 2321, Santa
Fe, New Mexico 87504-2321.

FIRST EDITION

10 9 8 7 6 5 4 3 2 1

Library of Congress Cataloging in Publication Data:
Schonberg, Leonard, 1935-
    Deadly Indian summer: a novel / by Leonard Schonberg.
        p. cm.
    ISBN: 0-86534-257-1 (hardcover)
    I. Title.
PS3569. C5258D4   1997
813'.54—dc21   96-48326
                                          CIP

Published by   SUNSTONE PRESS
                    Post Office Box 2321
                    Santa Fe, NM 87504-2321 / USA
                    (505) 988-4418 / orders only (800) 243-5644
                    FAX (505) 988-1025

FOR MY SONS

MY BROTHERS, a time of testing has come for us all.
We must believe everything or deny everything.
And who among you, I ask, would dare to deny everything?
                                        —Albert Camus
                                        The Plague

CHAPTER 1 _____

JOHN HARTMAN YAWNED AS HE CHANGED INTO scrubs and put on his lab coat. He had always been an early riser and liked being on the peds floor by seven to begin his rounds. On this particular morning the dawn could not shake itself loose from the grip of night. He stared out the window of the third floor doctors' lounge. The Indian Medical Center was situated on high ground and ordinarily afforded a good view of the town, but today it, along with the rest of Gallup, was wrapped in the brown shroud of a duststorm.

The morning's funereal gloom had a depressing effect on John's mood. He found himself suddenly immersed in memories that were so painful his head began to ache. He slumped down onto the sofa opposite the lockers and leaned his head back.

With his eyes closed to the glare of the overhead light bulb, he could imagine himself lying on Coronado beach beneath the summer sun of San Diego. Valentina was at his side, her presence so strong that he could smell the cinnamon fragrance of her skin and taste the salt spray on her lips. She wore a flowered maternity dress and as she lay on her back, John moved his hand gently over her rounded abdomen. He felt the baby kick against his fingers. Nuzzling Valentina's neck, he whispered into her ear how much he loved her. One small tear forced itself out of the corner of her eye. She smiled wistfully and fell asleep.

Later, walking back through the wet sand, John watched the watery circles spreading around their feet. Stopping for a moment, he reached down and with his finger traced a large heart with their names written in the center. Valentina smiled and kissed his cheek. Looking back as they continued walking, John saw the surf come pounding in, the waves obliterating his drawing.

The next night Dr. Brady called him at home and told him Valentina was in labor. He had admitted her to Otai Memorial and she had requested that John be called. John told his wife that he had to do an emergency consultation at the hospital. Janet never looked up from the book she was reading.

Driving to the hospital, John thought of the predicament he was in. He and Janet had been married almost four years before while he was in his internship in Boston. Janet was a commercial artist, as intent on her own career as John was on his. Deciding that New England was becoming too confining, John accepted a pediatrics residency at St. Luke's in San Diego. Janet was devastated. She had just been offered a position, an art directorship at one of the leading advertising agencies in New York. John realized he had acted impulsively and without consulting his wife, but the die was now cast and he couldn't go back on his agreement with St. Luke's. As time passed, John wondered whether he hadn't subconsciously created a situation that had to come to a head. Certainly he knew that he had dealt Janet's plans for advancement in her career a blow with this move. He also knew that every time he brought up the subject of children, Janet would steer the conversation back to the career track.

Life in San Diego drove a wedge into their relationship. He was happy with his residency program and enjoyed the proximity of the ocean and the absence of winter. Janet, on the other hand, could not find any meaningful work. For her, San Diego was "a city surrounded by ocean, Mexico, and boredom."

And then, in his second year of residency, he had met Valentina. She was an intensive care nurse at St. Luke's, also married. Their relationship had started innocently enough with lunch in the hospital coffee shop. It had progressed to lunch in a restaurant outside the hospital on her day off. It was a discovery period for both of them. Valentina talked about her childhood on the Texas border, where she was born, and her eventual move to California, where she had met her husband. She had seriously misjudged the man she married. Ray Hobbs, a San Diego County sheriff, had proven himself an insensitive brute whose greatest pleasure was "coming down hard on niggers and spics." At times he turned his wrath on Valentina and had given her a few bad beatings. They had now been married for three years and were childless.

"Why haven't you left him?" asked John.

"I guess I keep hoping for a miracle, hoping that he'll change. And I'm afraid of him."

John then unburdened himself, telling Valentina about the unhappy pall that had fallen over his own marriage.

"It looks like we've both made some mistakes," she responded.

As they left the restaurant, their hands joined and they smiled at one another.

"Can I see you again?" he asked.

"I'll be off next Tuesday," she said.

"I'll get someone to cover for me for part of the day," he answered. And then he surprised himself by asking "Would you like me to get a room for us?" His heart pounded as he posed the question and his face must have revealed his consternation because Valentina laughed.

"I'd like that very much," she answered.

And that was the beginning of a relationship that brought him more happiness and more emotional turmoil than he had ever known. All the passion absent in his life with Janet was expressed in his relationship with Valentina and she, in turn, gave herself to him with abandon. If Janet noticed anything different in their marriage, she gave no indication of it. And Ray Hobbs, as long as he found his dinner ready when he came home, didn't seem to care what Valentina did.

As the love between them intensified, they began to talk in earnest about what course of action to take. John felt that a separation between him and Janet was inevitable. He had begun his final year of residency and he knew Janet was only waiting for him to finish so that they could move back to the east coast. That was something he had no intention of doing, especially now that he was involved with Valentina.

Valentina, he knew, wanted out of her marriage but she lived in fear of her husband. More than once John had seen the bruises on her arms and chest and begged her to leave him. "He'll come after me," she said. And then she would cry in her helplessness.

With everything at an impasse, some serendipitous timing brought them a respite that renewed John's hopes that they would be able to work everything out. Ray Hobbs left for a week of hunting in Canada and Janet chose the same week to fly back east and visit her parents in Maine. John and Valentina had always acted circumspectly in the hospital, not wanting to draw any attention to themselves, but this was an opportunity that they had to take. Each of them arranged vacation days that week and they drove down to Ensenada, where they found a motel on the beach.

Their time in Ensenada could only be described as an idyll. When they weren't swimming or making love, they rented horses on the beach and rode along the water's edge. Watching Valentina with her hair flying in the wind and feeling the surge of his own's animal's flanks, John experienced an exhiliration he had never known. They spent their evenings walking along the edge of the bay, watching the fishing boats come in with their catch, and then they ate lobsters and crabs cooked on beach fires. The sunsets were spectacular and were followed by a giant moon that appeared to rise out of the stark hills of the Baja peninsula.

Trotting alongside Valentina on one of their afternoon rides, John told her he would like to marry her. "When?" she laughed, not thinking he was serious. "As soon as our divorces are final," he replied.

Valentina's face was radiant and as they returned the horses to the old man who tended them, she brought her mount next to John's and reached over to kiss him. Caught up in the dream-like existence in which they had lived for the past few days, Valentina excitedly told the old man that they were going to be married and asked him if he would like to come to the wedding. The old man grinned a toothless smile and they took him to a local cantina for a tequila to celebrate.

That night as they clung to one another in bed Valentina told him that she was pregnant and that the baby was his. John was now certain that nothing could stand in their way.

Reality intruded when they were back in San Diego and their spouses returned. The sense of freedom they had enjoyed in Ensenada dissipated and was again replaced by an ominous and oppressive feeling. Valentina was intimidated by Ray Hobbs' presence and John himself found it more difficult than he had anticipated to ask Janet for a divorce.

Month followed month and each of them maintained their precarious marriages. Valentina was perplexed by her husband's attitude. "He knows the baby isn't his and yet he doesn't seem to care," she told John. If anything, he had suddenly become solicitious of her, or at least no longer inflicted physical abuse.

Dr. Brady met John in the delivery suite at Otai Memorial.

"I understand you're a good friend of the family," he said. "Mrs. Hobbs would like you in the delivery room with her. Her labor is progressing rapidly so you'd better get your scrubs on."

John changed quickly and Valentina, already up in stirrups, looked at him as he entered the room. She started to smile but was interrupted by her next contraction. Her forehead glistened with perspiration and her knuckles turned white as she pulled back on the handles to help her bear down. John could already see the baby's black hair. He walked to the head of the table and stroked her forehead. Valentina wanted no anesthesia except a local if any stitches were needed.

"Come closer," she whispered. He bent down toward her. "I'm so happy I'm having your baby," she whispered. With the next pain, Valentina bore down and with a short yell pushed the baby out into Dr. Brady's waiting hands. It cried immediately.

"You have a daughter, Valentina," said Dr. Brady, holding the baby up for her to see after he had cut the cord.

"Congratulations, Valentina," John said, feeling awkward and not knowing what to do or say.

"To you, too." She mouthed the words at him, then closed her eyes.

"Well, John," said Dr. Brady, "since you're a friend of the family would you like to call Mr. Hobbs? Valentina said he was waiting at home for the news."

"I think it would be better if you called," John replied. "I've got to get back to St. Luke's to see a patient." He bent over and whispered into Valentina's ear. "Sleep well. I'll be up to see you tomorrow." She nodded, too tired to open her eyes or speak.

John drove home in a state of disbelief. He had a daughter but could not acknowledge the child as his. And what the future held for Valentina and him remained a big question mark. The one thing he was certain of was that their problems were no closer to being resolved.

The next day he drove down to Otai Memorial at noon. A tall, ruddy-faced blond man in a county sheriff's uniform walked out of

Valentina's room as John came down the corridor. The man paid him no attention but John's gaze was drawn to the holstered gun he wore on his hip.

Valentina was eating when he entered the room. She looked up with surprise. "Did you see Ray in the hall?" she asked.

John nodded. "If I had arrived a few minutes earlier he still would have been in the room."

"I just would have introduced you as one of the doctors. Besides, he should congratulate you," she said wickedly.

Although the other bed in the room was empty John looked around nervously. "There's no one sharing the room with you?"

"No, we're all alone, but I think it's too soon after the delivery, John."

They both laughed and after stealing a glance into the hall to make sure no one was around, John leaned over the bed and kissed her lips. Valentina threw her arms around his neck.

"I've missed you, my love. Are you happy?"

"I'm always happy when I'm with you."

"Have you seen the baby today?"

"I will on the way down. What did Ray say?"

"He said she was beautiful."

"Nothing more?"

"Ray is a man of few words. I'm sure that what he was saying was that I can go any time I want but the baby stays." With that, Valentina stared down at her tray and began to cry softly.

"Please, Val, don't. We'll work it out somehow. With time."

She shook her head. "No, John, I don't think we will."

He tried to reassure her but knew his words sounded as hollow to Valentina as they did to him.

She was discharged from the hospital on her third postpartum day. Ray Hobbs picked her and the baby up in the morning before John could get in to see them. On the following Sunday Valentina had the baby baptized. She was now Gabriella Maria Hobbs, nee Hartman. John sat in one of the rear pews but Valentina knew he was there.

With little more than two months remaining in the last year of his residency, John knew he no longer had the luxury of procrastination. A decision would have to be made. Janet was already pressuring him to set a date for their departure. "I don't care if it's a fellowship or private practice," she said, "but it's got to be New York or Boston."

To make matters worse, it was becoming more difficult to see Valentina. She had to depend on neighbors to even leave the house for a few minutes. John's own responsibilities at the hospital were also making it virtually impossible to get away during the day. During the first three weeks that Valentina was at home, they managed to see one another twice for only an hour, barely enough time to have a cup of coffee in a diner and steal a fast kiss. And John had not seen the baby at all since she left the hospital.

Valentina did not ask him what he intended to do when his residency ended. The question hung there between them, unasked and unanswered. Their telephone conversations, often strained, were a poor substitute for being together. John suggested that he come to the house to visit while her husband was out. It was risky but if he had his bag with him they could always pass it off as a pediatrics visit for the baby if Ray Hobbs showed up. John's first visit had them both on edge. He played with Gabriella for a few minutes, holding her and cooing at her, then stayed only for a cup of coffee. After that it became easier. John's hospital schedule eased and he visited Valentina two or three afternoons a week. She told him that Hobbs never returned home before eight in the evening and even then paid no attention to her. He focused entirely on the baby.

They became comfortable enough to hold one another and kiss, and from there it wasn't long before they were making love in Valentina's bed.

With only two weeks remaining in his residency program, John decided to tell Janet he was not returning to the east coast. In fact, he had not inquired about any fellowships or looked for any practice opportunities on either coast. He knew that Janet would leave anyway and that their marriage would end but that would permit him to concentrate on what he wanted to do and how best to resolve the situation with Valentina. More and more he believed that leaving San Diego with no forwarding address would be the only way they would be able to get away from Ray Hobbs. Perhaps then, with time, Hobbs would become more amenable to a divorce.

On the day that Gabriella was two months old, John decided to bring her a present. He found some colorful dresses in a downtown department store and headed for Valentina's house in Chula Vista.

She was delighted with the presents and picked out a yellow dress with flowers across the front to put on Gabriella. They strapped her in her infant chair and she watched them with her large brown eyes while they had coffee.

John told Valentina of his decision to speak to Janet that same evening and he watched the relief spread over her face. "And then," he added, "as soon as my residency is over we'll figure out how to get you away from Hobbs."

Laughing gaily now, Valentina put the baby in her crib for her nap and she and John fell into each other's arms on the bed. They made love, losing themselves completely, and for the first time in Valentina's house they fell asleep. John awoke with a start and looked at his watch. It was almost six. He jumped from the bed and rearranged his clothes.

"Don't worry," said Valentina, "he won't be home for another two hours."

"I hope the hospital hasn't been looking for me though."

"Do you want to call them?"

"No, Val, I'd better run. I can always give them a ring from a payphone. I'll let you know tomorrow how things go tonight."

They embraced at the door and kissed one more time. "Give Gabriella a kiss for her daddy," he said.

John saw her standing in the doorway as he drove away. She smiled and waved. He also caught a glimpse of a yellow car parked a short distance up the block from Valentina's house but paid it no heed. There was an Exxon station at the other end of the block and he headed there to use the phone.

As he began getting his messages from the St. Luke's operator he stared abstractedly through the booth's window. He found himself looking at something that bothered him but for a moment couldn't decide what it was. And then it struck him! The yellow car! The yellow car he had seen out of the corner of his eye when he left Valentina was now parked in front of her house. And at the instant he realized it was a sheriff's cruiser, he heard three loud noises like firecrackers going off.

People in the station were looking up the block. The operator continued reading off her messages but John no longer listened. His heart pounded and he had a metallic taste in his mouth. Letting the telephone drop and dangle from its cord, he pulled the door open and ran back to Valentina's house. Some of her neighbors had come out of their homes and were looking at the house and at one another. They watched John as he breathlessly ran up to the door. He listened outside for a moment but there was only a heavy silence. He pushed at the door and it swung open. A few neighbors crowded behind him and tried to peer in. The front entrance looked into the kitchen and John could see their coffee cups still on the table. A chill passed through him and he found it difficult to breathe. Turning the first corner he looked into the living room. It was empty. But in the bedroom he found Valentina sprawled on the bed, her mouth open in a grimace with a trickle of blood coursing down her chin. There was a large bloody spot on the front of her blouse. Ray Hobbs was on the floor. Matted hair, blood, and bone fragments deformed one side of his head and a large puddle of blood had formed under him. The gun was near his hand. John staggered to the crib. Gabriella's pretty yellow dress was soaked in blood and her skin looked like marble. Hobbs had killed them all.

John heard a woman behind him scream. There was a ringing in his ears and then he remembered nothing else. When he awoke he was lying on the sofa and two policemen were looking down at him.

"How do you feel?" one of them asked.

"I don't know. Where am I?" He looked around—and then he remembered. Valentina's living room was filled with police. A middle-aged man in a brown suit sat down on the edge of the sofa as John struggled into a sitting position.

"Would you like to tell us what happened? I'm Detective Keats."

"Are they all dead?" he asked, already knowing the answer. Keats nodded.

John cried, unable to speak, and Keats waited patiently. And then John told him about Valentina and Ray Hobbs, and about Gabriella and Janet. A man nearby scribbled on a pad as he spoke. "He should have killed me and let them live," said John. "It's all my fault for waiting too long. I should have done something sooner."

"I wouldn't be so hard on myself, doc," said the man in the brown suit. "Mrs. Hobbs knew what she was dealing with. She should have left him and gotten a restraining order to keep him away from her. You may have made some mistakes—but you didn't pull the trigger."

"It was the same as if I did."

Keats leaned forward and fixed him with an intent stare. "Doc, I've been a cop for thirty years and there's one thing I can tell you. Things are going to be tough for a while. You're going to find that people can be bastards. So if I were you I'd stop blaming myself. You're going to need all the strength you've got to fight back and see this through. They eventually forget—but in the meantime it's going to be hell. I suggest you head home and try to get some sleep. Just don't plan on going anywhere without letting us know. We may need to talk to you again while we're finishing our investigation."

It was dark when John left the house. People milled about outside and they watched him as he walked down the block back to the gas station. His car was still parked next to the phone booth. He sat down in the driver's seat and looked at his watch. It was ten o'clock, four hours since he had left Valentina and Gabriella, four hours since their lives had ended. He found himself crying again. It was something he was going to do a lot of for many weeks.

When he arrived back at his apartment, his suitcases were standing outside the door. There was a letter on top of them with his name on it.

It was obvious that the news had travelled quickly. Janet informed him that she was leaving within a day or two and that he was not to try to see her. He would be hearing from her lawyer. He raised his hand to knock on the door, then thought better of it. There was nothing he could say to her. He picked up his bags and carried them to the car.

John spent the night in a motel, sleeping fitfully and then lying awake until the first purple streaks of dawn appeared in the sky. He decided he would have to go to the hospital to work as usual. Although he dreaded facing everyone, he still had his responsibilities to the sick kids on the ward.

Looking into the bathroom mirror, he had difficulty recognizing himself. He was unshaven, his eyes swollen and glazed and his skin lined with wrinkles he had never seen before. He felt he had aged ten years. After forcing down two cups of black coffee in a local diner, he drove to St. Luke's.

It was early and the seven o'clock change of shifts had not yet taken place. The few people John encountered stared at him with surprise. It was apparent that the news had reached the hospital. He took the elevator up to the housestaff sleeping rooms to try to borrow a razor. The first person he saw was Larry Gordon, a second-year surgical resident.

"Jesus, John, you look like hell. And I thought I had a bad night."

Larry rattled on about his admissions and John thought he must be the only one who hadn't heard anything. He borrowed his razor and shaved, biting his lip through the entire process to prevent himself from bursting into tears. He found that he hated looking at his own face in the mirror.

When he reached the pediatrics ward there were no good-mornings from the nurses and clerks. They all avoided eye contact and acted as though he wasn't there. John remembered the detective's words as he picked up his charts.

The mother of one of his seriously ill asthmatic children was sitting next to her son's bed when John entered the room. She stood up when she saw him.

"Dr. Hartman, I saw the news on the television. I'm so sorry to hear what happened."

John dissolved in tears and the woman put her arms around him and held him. That was the only expression of sympathy John was to receive that day or in his final week at the hospital.

Later that morning John was called to the office of the hospital administrator, Stuart Robbins. His relationship with Robbins had always been friendly but today there was only cold formality. "Sit down, Doctor," said Robbins. "Your performance in your entire three years of residency has been beyond reproach—until this unfortunate occurrence."

John felt like screaming 'the unfortunate occurrence is the death of the woman I loved and my child' but he bowed his head and said nothing.

"I don't know what your plans are, Dr. Hartman, whether or not you intend to practice in San Diego or move on. But in view of the situation, I want to advise you that if you do intend to practice here, an application for privileges would not be looked upon favorably. If you intend to go elsewhere, you will receive an excellent recommendation for your work as a resident. Do I make myself clear?"

"I have no intention of remaining in San Diego," John said,

rising from his chair. And that was the end of the discussion, his final leave-taking from St. Luke's.

There was only one item of unfinished business. He called Detective Keats and asked if he had any information about the funeral.

"We've reached Mrs. Hobbs' parents in San Antonio. Mr. Hobbs had no immediate family. Mrs. Hobbs' family will be arriving today to arrange the funeral. They'll have a hard enough time facing this, Doc, and in view of the situation, I don't think you should plan on attending the services."

John opened his eyes and pushed himself up from the sofa. He took out his wallet and looked at the photograph of Valentina taken on the beach in Ensenada. Even now, after three years with the Indian Health Service in Gallup, he had not been able to dull his pain. He still felt he had failed Valentina in death as well as in life.

CHAPTER 2 _____

SWIRLING CLOUDS OF BROWN DUST DRIVEN BY desert winds swept across the interstate and blotted out the New Mexico landscape that Sam Spencer longed to see after so many years. The looming plateaus and sweeping expanse of desert that he knew were out there and looked to for solace on this June morning were totally obscured in the oppressive darkness.

The previous afternoon, at Julia's funeral, he had thought if he left Flagstaff early enough he would reach New Mexico as the sun came up. He would see the hills framed by the red streaks of sunrise and the rays streaming into his car would be like a rebirth, helping him escape from the memories brought back by being in Flagstaff and seeing Kate's mother laid to rest. Instead, he found himself reimmersed in the gloomy remembrances of yesterday, thinking of Kate and Jeff and another funeral that he always fought so desperately to keep from his consciousness.

Probing beams of light from the sparse oncoming traffic pierced the brown fog, and tumbleweed, hurtling ahead of the wind and appearing suddenly in front of the car, was disconcerting enough to cause his foot to hit the brake more than once that morning. Each time, he thought an animal had suddenly lunged out of the darkness.

He stole a glance at his watch. Eight o'clock. It was hard to believe. The night had been clear and filled with stars when he left Flagstaff and it was only when he reached a point midway between Holbrook and Gallup that the winds had started. By the time he arrived at the New Mexico border it was necessary to roll up the car window to keep from choking on the dust.

The last roadsign he had seen indicated that Gallup lay only a few miles ahead. He hoped it wouldn't be necessary to drive all the way to Albuquerque under these intolerable conditions.

The wind squalls danced on every side of him, occasionally shifting direction and driving the sand directly into the windshield. It was impossible to see now without running the windshield wipers. He watched the sand accumulate along the edges of the wiper blades and listened to their steady rhythmic thump. His mind's eye watched the minister sprinkling earth on Julia's coffin and he heard the steady scraping sound of shovels.

It was only two days ago that the past forcibly intruded on his life with the phone call from Kate's sister, Evelyn. Even when Kate was alive there had been little communication with Evelyn and now, ten years after Kate's death, he was unable to even remember what Evelyn looked like. Her brusque, clipped speech, however, was unmistakable.

She wasted no time on pleasantries, barely giving him time to get over his astonishment. "Julia died this morning, Sam. I know you were close to her and thought you might want to attend the funeral in Flagstaff tomorrow. Of course, I realize how busy you are."

He had thanked her for being considerate enough to call and promised to attend. It was all very simple, very formal. His plane ticket from Washington to Phoenix was purchased that same day and he was on American's night flight, arriving the following morning in time to rent a car and drive to Flagstaff.

He still could not understand why he never considered not going. It was certainly true that he had been close to Julia. During the twelve years that he and Kate were married, he never thought of her as a mother-in-law. She was too dynamic a woman to label so conventionally. For forty years, she had been a practicing attorney in Flagstaff, devoting herself to Native American causes long before it became fashionable.

His first meeting with her was vividly clear in his mind. It was after he and Kate had decided to get married.

"Well, Mr. Spencer," she said curtly, but with an undisguised twinkle in her clear blue eyes, "I understand you want to marry my daughter. Kate also tells me you're an attorney." He had worn his most conservative grey suit for the meeting and she looked him up and down. Before he could reply, she went on. "I do hope you're not one of those stuffy Ivy League types."

He was speechless but Kate only laughed.

"Being an attorney, Mr.Spencer, is a rather abominable profession. My late husband would have told you that since he had enough experience living with one. But it happens to be the work I love and it's all what you make of it. I'm sure you feel the same way.

"I've brought up my two daughters to think for themselves. If you know Kate, that must be apparent. And if Kate wants to marry you..." She paused and her face broke into a smile. "That's good enough for me," she said, extending her hand and shaking his firmly.

Yes, he had admired her and felt close to her. It was possible to talk about anything with Julia—and she was tolerant enough to overlook the fact that her judgement had been discerning. He was, in truth, a stuffy Ivy Leage type, more so in those early days when he was just a few years out of Harvard Law School.

But that was all so long ago. And once Kate was gone, his relationship with Julia had ended. That was not her choice. She had tried to maintain the friendship between them, but for him to come to terms with the death of Kate and Jeff he had had to totally dissociate himself from anything that reminded him of them. He was sure that Julia understood and for ten years, until the call from Evelyn, she had been effectively divorced from his thoughts.

Then why go back now for the funeral when it no longer mattered?

Evelyn had given him an out—he certainly was busy, especially with the peace talks only a week away. There was absolute pandemonium at State with last minute details and he himself had been meeting with the President on almost a daily basis. To absent himself for even two days at this point would not be wise—nor looked upon very favorably by the parties concerned.

"It must be that ridiculous streak of sentimentality I've never been able to cure myself of," he said in the Oval Office the afternoon of Evelyn's call, not believing for a moment that that was the case.

The President was in no mood to be tolerant. "Then it's about time you got rid of that streak or whatever you call it. Jesus, Sam, this is no time to be running all over the country. The talks are only a week away and you know how much remains to be done."

In the end, he had reluctantly given his Secretary of State forty-eight hours. Of course, the President had been unaware of Sam's decision to use commercial transportation and dispense with his Secret Service protection. It was, Sam knew, an indefensible action for which he would catch hell upon his return. But if it was impossible to explain his decision to attend Julia's funeral, how much more difficult it would have been to justify his desire to be alone on this trip.

The thought of the forty-eight hours he had been allotted made him again look anxiously at his watch. Christ, he thought, what if it's like this all the way to Albuquerque? And what if there are no flights going out in this wind? To make matters worse, he had been given a car with a radio that did not function, precluding any possibility of finding out what the weather was like elsewhere in the state or of receiving any news emanating from Washington.

He had intentionally chosen to drive the rental car to Albuquerque rather than back to Phoenix. It was beginning to look like that was a serious misjudgement on his part but the pace of the past few months had been almost beyond his endurance. With the added strain of having to confront the past again, he thought that the ride would help to restore his equilibrium—it was to be, after all, only a few stolen hours, a short time to indulge himself in the beauty of a sunrise over the New Mexico desert. His flight was scheduled to leave at two in the afternoon and he had given himself more than enough time to make the drive. But now, with the storm...

His hands tightened with anger and frustration on the steering wheel. Nothing had gone right. He cursed himself for his stupidity in going to the funeral and he swore at the desert and the wind for ruining the morning he had longed for.

Strength of mind was Sam Spencer's credo. Absolute control over one's emotions and total dedication to one's work were the watchwords he lived by. In the ten years since Kate's death he had sustained himself by adhering to these principles. Not only had he been able to endure the shock of losing his family, he had persevered and gained new strengths that led him to his present position. He was, after all, not yet fifty and had gone from U.S. attorney, the position he held at the time of Kate's death, to professor of international law, and now to Secretary of State.

Although he knew that sentimentality did not enter into his decision to return for Julia's funeral, he could not have offered any other reason to the President since he himself did not understand his decision to attend.

For Sam Spencer to be at the mercy of a whim, or to follow a course of action that was not thought through, was entirely out of character. It was this deviation from customary behavior that nagged at Sam all through the trip.

Evelyn had been waiting for him at the cemetery gate. "Hello, Sam," she said simply, extending her hand. "I'm glad you could come. It was good of you."

"It's good to see you, Evelyn. I'm terribly sorry about your mother. She was a wonderful woman."

Evelyn nodded and they walked along the path in silence. His words sounded hollow and he felt himself in the presence of a stranger. The woman at his side looked something like the image he retained of Julia, small and slender with dark, grey-streaked hair and an almost regal bearing, but it was as if he were meeting her for the first time. He wondered, too, whether there was any resemblance to Kate, but he could no longer remember with certainty what his wife had looked like. One of the first things he had done after her death was to pack all their pictures away in a box, which still remained sealed.

Several people at the gravesite approached him and shook his hand. Some looked vaguely familiar but he could not place them. Although Julia had had a small family, he and Kate had not had time for much contact with them.

During the eulogy his gaze wandered over the immaculate green fields with their crosses and monuments. The low-lying hills at the outskirts of the cemetery gradually ascended and metamorphosed into an evergreen forest. A hawk circled lazily over the tree line describing its aimless circles on the turquoise sky.

"...we will always remember her kindness...an inspiration... friends and family..."

The words of the minister's oration drifted in and out of his consciousness. He was aware only of the sun on his face and the faintest trace of a summer breeze that danced delicately upon his skin. Then he heard the minister's handful of earth hitting the coffin.

"...ashes to ashes, dust to dust..."

The small processional walked away from the grave and as they approached the entrance he could hear the sound of shoveling in the distance.

He abruptly decided that he had felt nothing. The funeral had been merely a ceremony that he watched with the same detachment he brought to official functions at the State Department. Julia remained a distant memory. Evelyn and the others were strangers. The goodbyes at the gate were perfunctory and polite. Once again he shook hands with Evelyn and mumbled his condolences, but he was aware now of his conscious effort to avoid her gaze.

It was not until he drove away and felt a tightening in his throat that he realized a crack had occurred in his defenses. The pine-covered hills, the neatly arranged markers, the heads lowered at the graveside—all had made their impression and triggered emotions that now struggled for release. He pulled off the road, his body trembling and his breathing constricted.

"Oh, God, not after all this time," he moaned. "Damn, damn, damn..." He muttered the word over and over, struggling to regain his composure.

The one image against whose recall he had unconsciously fought since his arrival at the cemetery blinded him now with its intensity. Placed side by side were two headstones. One bore the name "Catherine Morrow Spencer" and the other "Jeffrey Robert Spencer." He visualized their exact location in the cemetery, not far removed from where Julia now rested, and suddenly he felt a surge of shame. Was he such a coward then, a traitor to the memory of the only two people he had ever loved, that he could not bring himself to even visit their graves?

Not since that most dismal day of his life ten years earlier had he returned to the spot where Kate and Jeff lay buried. All the defenses he had erected, all the rationalizations, now crumbled away and he knew he would have to go back.

It took him only a few minutes to drive back to the entrance. The mourners who had been at Julia's funeral were gone and, except for an occasional groundsman, the cemetery stretched out deserted before him. He retraced the same path he had walked earlier, a purposefulness in his stride now that all hesitation had been swept aside by the force of his decision. Not more than a hundred feet in front of him he could see the men still filling the grave that contained Julia's coffin. A path veered off to the right and he followed it automatically, his steps now directed by a memory that had lain dormant for years but was as fresh as yesterday. The grass in this section of the cemetery appeared to have been freshly cut and the sweet fragrance imposed itself on his senses. He watched a small yellow butterfly fluttering from tombstone to tombstone, pausing for only a brief second on each slab.

His gaze was fixed now on two stones still a short distance ahead of him. The determination of his steps gave way suddenly to an indecisive lethargy. His legs moved slowly, almost in opposition to the rest of his body. And then he was there, once more confronting the last earthly traces of his wife and son. The names on the stones leaped out at him, beating their way into a consciousness now receptive to them. No longer in control of his legs, he slumped to his knees on the manicured grass and wept uncontrollably.

He winced now at the memory of his behavior. What good was it for himself or for Kate and Jeff? What was the sense of remembering and feeling? There was no way to retrieve the past. When he had driven away from the cemetery for the second time, he felt only repugnance for his actions. The great catharsis, he realized, was more one of anger than of relief. The senselessness of the deaths of Kate and Jeff and the bitterness it was capable of arousing in him were no less true now than at the time of the accident.

The piercing whistle of a Santa Fe train startled him. The engine moved slowly by on his left, one car after another then appearing suddenly from behind the wind-whipped curtain of sand. On his own side of the road he could dimly see the beginnings of Gallup's motel strip. He decided then to get off the interstate and take the main road through town. It would give him the chance to get a cup of coffee and call the airlines to see if he could expect a delay at Albuquerque's airport. Traffic on Sixty-six was still light despite the fact that no one seemed to be moving faster than thirty-five miles an hour. He fished his pipe and tobacco out of his jacket and filled the bowl while resting his wrists on the steering wheel. Suddenly, tail-lights that he had not seen before appeared directly in front of him. Sam hit his brakes hard while grabbing for the wheel, spilling the contents of his tobacco pouch into his lap.

"Damn!" he exclaimed. "The jackass is stopped in the middle of the road."

He started to pass on the left, then applied his brakes again when he noticed the car in the opposing lane was also stopped. An indistinct mass was lying on the road between the two vehicles. He put on his emergency blinker and stepped out into a blast of wind that almost tore the door out of his hand. Shielding his eyes as best he could, he moved forward and saw the body of a large animal. When he had almost reached it he saw that it was a horse, its belly torn open and a mass of steaming intestines protruding. The beast was still breathing, its eyes staring in fright and its nostrils quivering. There was broken glass on the road and now, for the first time, he noticed the front end of the car facing him was smashed. The driver still sat in the car.

Sam leaned into the wind and approached the man, whose window was rolled up.

"Are you all right?" he called, rapping on the glass.

The man stared at him vacantly, then slowly began to roll down the window. He was white-haired and appeared to be about seventy. Sam could see the confusion on his face.

"What happened? Did I hit something?"

"You hit a horse."

Sam wondered why he himself had not heard it happen since it must have occurred only moments before he arrived at the spot, but with the wind blowing and the car windows rolled up it was understandable.

The light came back into the old man's eyes as he remembered.

"That's it! I couldn't hardly see anything with the goddamn sand everywhere and then suddenly a horse runs in front of me. I hit the brake but I guess it was too late." He pushed open the car door and got out to look. "Hell, it must be wild or runaway. Ain't even got a saddle."

Traffic was starting to back up now in both directions and a few horns competed with the roar of the wind. Sam looked to where the other car was stopped and could see figures gathered on the far side. They looked like ghostly apparitions in the murky light and were staring at something on the ground. Sam walked over and could see a small figure on the road surrounded by a circle of men. Except for one grizzled, leather-skinned white man wearing a stetson, everyone else was Indian. The smell of whiskey was heavy in the air and some of the men were having difficulty standing.

"What happened?" asked Sam.

The white man squinted at him. "Damned if I know. Craziest thing I ever seen. This injun kid was riding along on his horse, then suddenly the kid falls off, just keels over like, and the horse spooks and runs out into the middle of the highway and gets hisself hit by a car. I'm lucky I seed what happened or I could have run over this kid laying in the road. It's darker than hell out here with all that sand blowing."

Sam kneeled down to look at the boy. He was about ten or eleven and lay on his back, very still except for the movements of his labored breathing. His face was sweating and flushed with strands of his shoulder length hair stuck to his cheeks. From his partially opened lips came a gurgling sound with every exhalation. Sam kept one hand raised to his eyes to keep the sand from blinding him and with the other felt the boy's head, looking for any obvious injury. He wondered if the boy's unconscious state might be from some type of epileptic condition. When his palm touched the youth's forehead, he reacted with surprise.

"This kid's burning up with fever." He looked up at the men surrounding him. "Is there a hospital we could take him to?"

The Indians looked at one another, then stared impassively at him. A few wandered off to join a line which Sam now saw for the first time in front of an unopened saloon. He noticed, too, that some Indians were sprawled on the sidewalk.

The man in the stetson giggled hoarsely. "Sheeet, you ain't gonna get any help from them. It's almost nine o'clock and that means the saloon's going to open."

"We can't just leave the kid here," argued Sam. "Don't you know a hospital or doctor where we can take him?"

Sam heard himself almost yelling, trying to overcome the noise of the wind and car horns. Some of the traffic now snaked around on both shoulders of the road, pausing only momentarily to see what was going on. The other old man had finished looking at the horse and at the damage to his car and now joined them. He looked down at the boy, then at Sam. "Is the kid dead? I don't remember hitting no kid."

"The boy is sick," Sam replied. "We've got to get him to a hospital."

He could not believe the indifference of these people and felt his anger rising. "Well, goddamn it, we can't just stand here. Someone call the police. We've got a sick kid and a horse that needs to be put out of its misery."

At the mention of the word "police", a few more of the Indians drifted away. The two white men stared at him strangely as if to say "why are you getting so excited?"

The man with the stetson was the first to speak again. "You could take him to the Indian Hilton."

"To the what?"

"The Indian Hilton."

The other man snickered, apparently recovered enough from his earlier confusion to appreciate the joke. "That's the Indian hospital," he said. "It's not too far from here."

"Well, if you know where it is can you drive the boy there?"

The man rubbed his chin. "I'd better wait here for the patrol boys to arrive. They might not like me leaving after hitting the horse. Besides, I gotta find out who's gonna pay for me bustin' my headlight. If that's the kid's horse, then his folks'll have to pay me."

"But you killed the horse," said Sam, aghast at what he was listening to.

"Well, if the kid can't control his animal that ain't no fault of mine."

"Look," said Sam sharply, facing the other man. "I've got to catch a plane in Albuquerque. Can you take this boy to the hospital?"

"I'd like to help you out, mister, but I'm late for work already. It'll only take you a few minutes. Just go down the road to Second Street and make a right. You follow Second into Highway 32 till you get to Nizhoni. You can't miss the place. It's bigger'n anything else."

Sam opened his mouth to argue, then looked again at the boy. Glaring at the two men, he lifted the child in his arms and carried him to his car. The boy was light in his arms and Sam realized it had been a long time since he last held a child. He placed him on the front passenger seat and then, after entering from the driver's side, he propped the boy against the opposite door.

The man in the stetson had already driven away and the road in front of him was now clear. Sam drove slowly past the body of the horse and saw the old white-haired man staring in rapt fascination at the shuddering flanks of the animal, now in its final death throes. His hands were thrust deeply into his pockets while the sand swirled about him and he took no notice of Sam's departure.

Sam drove past the pawn shops and motels watching for the Second Street sign. The boy had now begun to cough. His entire body shook and Sam had to reach out his arm to keep him from falling forward against the dashboard. The seizure of coughing continued and suddenly the boy's eyes opened in fright. His face was contorted and he gasped and uttered short cries in his frantic effort to breathe.

"Easy, son, easy," said Sam, "I'm taking you to the hospital."

He tried to watch the road and the boy at the same time and was afraid he would miss the turnoff. The coughing fit had subsided and the boy once again appeared to be asleep or unconscious. His parched lips were open and Sam reached out to touch his forehead again. It was burning. Christ, this kid is sick, he said to himself.

The street sign on the corner said "Eighth" and he watched now as the numbers descended. Second came up quickly and he turned into the street, following it uphill, past the shabby homes with their dirty yards of brown earth and sand. At least some of the wind-blown sand was blocked here and he could read the street signs more easily.

The monotonous brown and white stucco houses appeared to be an outgrowth of the very ground upon which they stood. There was no grass, no trees, no flowers. Nature, in bestowing her blessings, had simply passed Gallup by and its inhabitants had apparently accepted their lot. Sam remembered that the town was a major trade center for the surrounding reservations, its economic life guided by the white traders who ran the Indian crafts shops. For the travelers who passed through following the interstate or 66, Gallup was simply a place to buy a squash-blossom necklace or a cup of coffee. For the Indians, who made up the bulk of its population, it was Nuni-Shozy, or Iron Bridge, a place to get some menial work or pawn their valuables or drink. Alcohol was forbidden on the Navajo reservation and the Indians came to Gallup to drown the misery of their existence in the bottles of cheap whiskey and wine which they guzzled in the saloons and on the street corners.

Second Street had become State Highway 32 and in the distance, off to the left, Sam could see a large white building of four or five floors. The street that led to the structure was Nizhoni and he turned left into it. He could see why the men had derisively referred to it as the "Indian Hilton." It was, from the outside at least, a large relatively new hospital and the only modern building he had seen in the town. He could imagine the anger of the Anglos when the Indian Health Service built this imposing facility for the Indians.

He looked at his watch again as he drove into the hospital parking lot. It was nine o'clock. Well, he had more to do than worry about Anglos and Indians and their differences. He had a plane to catch. Sam turned sharply into the only empty space in a long line of parked pickup trucks and cars that had seen better days.

The boy had begun to cough again and was gagging on the secretions rattling in his throat. Sam quickly picked him up and looked nervously at the blue color of his lips. He walked hurriedly to the main entrance, squeezing past Indian women blocking the doorway, and entered the building.

There were Indians everywhere, filling the rows of seats in the lobby, leaning against the walls, squatting in corners, and filing up and down the corridors in the company of nurses and doctors. Some of the men wore standard western garb of denims, flannel shirts, and stetsons; others wore more urban Anglo style slacks and shirts with bola ties. The women's dress varied from the traditional full calico skirts and velveteen blouses to more fashionable short skirts. A few of the men wore their hair long, in braids or pony tails, while the women, no matter how poor and tattered their clothes, all wore exquisite silver and turquoise jewelry in the form of bracelets, rings and necklaces.

Many children were also present, ranging from infants in their mother's arms or on cradle boards to almond-eyed boys and girls of school age. The majority were sneezing and coughing but otherwise sat quietly in their seats.

Sam walked up to the registration desk, followed by the curious stares of all the people. The three young women working at the desk were all Indian. They looked with surprise at the tall, conservatively dressed white man carrying an Indian boy in his arms.

"I have a very sick boy here. Can I see the doctor, please."

"Yes, one moment please" said a soft-spoken woman with wire-rimmed glasses. She moved out from behind the desk and motioned to Sam. "Would you follow me, please."

She led him down a corridor filled with patients and nurses coming and going in both directions. For the large number of patients in the waiting area, there appeared to be far too few examining rooms.

A woman walked out of one of the rooms carrying a small child whose face was ravaged by impetigo. The bespectacled woman leading Sam said something quickly in Navajo to which the other woman responded with a nod. Sam was then taken into a small cubicle, barely large enough to contain an examining table, a supply cabinet, and a miniscule desk, seated in front of which was a dark-haired young physician entering notes on a patient record.

"Excuse me, Doctor Hartman, we have an emergency," said the Indian woman.

John Hartman swung around in his chair and his face registered surprise when he looked at Sam. The only time the hospital had visitors with so dignified an appearance was when bureaucrats from the Bureau of Indian Affairs or the Indian Health Service visited on official inspection tours.

Having done his undergraduate work at Yale, John was certain as he looked at the tall, grey-haired man in front of him that he could detect Ivy League and his first guess was Harvard. Something about the man's bearing, the cut of his clothes, and the straightforwardness with which he looked John in the eye suggested not only his background, but the importance of his position. Not even his windblown appearance and the sand that coated his dark suit detracted from the impression. There was also something familiar about the face and John was certain he had seen this man before.

Sam nodded at the small body in his arms. "Shall I put him on the table?"

"Yes, of course." John stood up and looked at the Indian boy. He could see at a glance that the child was acutely ill.

"Can you tell me what happened?"

"I picked him up on the highway near the edge of town. From what I could learn he had fallen off his horse. The horse must have gotten frightened and bolted. It was hit by a car and it's back there on the road."

"Was the boy hit also?"

"I don't believe so. He seems to have a high fever and difficulty breathing."

John turned to the woman who had led Sam in.

"Sally, would you ask one of the nurses to come in and help me get the boy undressed."

As she left the room, John placed one hand on the boy's head and with the other checked his pulse. At that moment, the boy groaned and once again had a coughing fit that threatened to strangle him. He tried to sit up, then fell back and lapsed once more into unconsciousness. Brown-flecked saliva dribbled from one corner of his mouth.

"This child is really sick," he said to the nurse who had just entered. "Let's get his clothes off fast."

The nurse was a middle-aged black woman who clucked commiseratingly as she gently removed the boy's worn and patched denims. "He's burning up," she said, throwing an anxious glance at John.

While she put a temperature patch on the boy's forehead, John rolled him on his side and listened to his lungs. "We've been seeing a lot of respiratory crud, Emma, but nothing this bad." The nurse nodded.

John turned then to Sam. "It was good of you to bring the boy in. There are many Anglos here who wouldn't have bothered."

"Indians, too," replied Sam. "The bars were getting ready to open."

John nodded understandingly, then extended his hand. "Incidentally, I'm John Hartman. I run the pediatric service."

"I'm Sam Spencer."

John's eyes opened wide in a flash of recognition. "I knew I had seen you before—on TV and in newspapers. You're the Secretary of State!" he blurted in disbelief. "But I don't understand. What are you doing here in Gallup?"

"It's a long story," said Sam, amused at the looks he was getting from the doctor and nurse, but feeling somewhat embarrassed at the same time.

Before either of them could say anything more, Emma checked the temperature patch. "One hundred six," she said softly.

"Emma, let's get an IV going with point nine saline while I check him over. And ask Sally to put in a call for the lab tech stat. After that we'll get him over to X-Ray for a chest film."

The nurse returned moments later with a bottle of intravenous fluid. While she inserted the needle in the boy's arm and started the drip, John Hartman worked methodically, examining every part of the child's body. Sam knew he should be leaving to continue his drive but was reluctant to interrupt John's examination. He was about to leave the room to look for a payphone when another physician entered.

"What do you have, John?"

"This kid's in trouble, Bill. Temp 106, comatose, cyanotic. He's got a 140 tach and his pressure is low. Lungs have rhonchi and wheezes and his sputum looks blood-tinged. He's also got nodes in his neck and left axilla."

"Do you think it's all respiratory?"

"Well, my first guess would be a severe pneumonitis. TB is always a possibility, too. But something bothers me about this—this kid is almost too toxic to have either of those."

"What's your plan?"

"After the lab work and cultures are done, I'll get a chest film and then start him on IV Tetracycline empirically."

"Sounds good to me."

At that moment, the technician, a young Mexican girl who looked no older than sixteen, appeared in the doorway.

"Come on in, Lee," called John. "We want a CBC, chemistries, blood culture and cultures of his sputum. Have them run the bloods stat."

She prepared her tubes and syringes and while she drew the blood she needed, John introduced the newly arrived physician to Sam.

"This is Bill Moore, our chief of medicine. Bill, this is Mr. Spencer—Sam Spencer. He found the boy on the road and brought him in here."

Sam extended his hand to the young, freckle-faced man who peered at him quizzically. "Not *the* Sam Spencer?"

"I'm afraid so."

Bill Moore grinned. "Did you lose your way while travelling to Damascus or has Gallup suddenly become a political hot spot?"

"Bill's our local comedian," said John, staring at his friend reproachfully.

"I'm through, Doctor," interrupted the lab technician, depositing the last tubes in her basket.

"Thanks, Lee. Have the lab page me as soon as soon as they have any results."

"Excuse me, Dr. Hartman," said Sam. "I'm supposed to catch a two o'clock flight out of Albuquerque. Is there a phone I can use to call the airline to see if there's any delay because of the sandstorm?"

"Sure. I'll take you down to the Administrator's office. Emma, take the boy to X-Ray for the chest film. Then give him 500 milligrams of Tetracycline IV and take him up to the ward. Tell the nurses on the floor I'll be up shortly to write orders. He can be admitted as John Doe for now."

Sam was about to say his goodbyes to the others in the room when the boy began to groan and toss restlessly. His eyes opened briefly and he mumbled something unintelligible, then had another short fit of coughing. This time a small amount of bright red sputum spattered on the floor.

"Emma, you better tell the nurses on the ward to isolate him and take respiratory precautions," said John. "Also, have them put a peds cath tray and a lumbar puncture tray in his room."

He turned to Bill Moore. "Bill, do you mind staying with Emma and the boy until I get back?"

"No problem. Nice meeting you, Mr. Spencer," he said. "And I wish you well with the peace talks. But tell Washington to leave a little money for the Indian Health Service." The two men shook hands and Sam followed John Hartman out of the room.

"Nothing subtle about Bill," said John.

"Look, Dr. Hartman, I know how busy you are and how seriously ill the boy is. I don't want to take you away from your work. If you'd just tell me where the nearest payphone is, I'm sure—"

They were interrupted by a stretcher being wheeled down the corridor toward them.

"Room three," called John, waving to the orderly.

"Excuse me for a second," he said to Sam and stopped at the front desk. He called to the young woman who had led Sam to the examining room. "He's being admitted to Peds isolation, Sally. John Doe, for now."

Sam, still feeling himself a burden, tried again to extricate himself but John interrupted him. "Mr. Spencer, if Russell Oliver, our esteemed administrator, found out that you had graced this hospital with a visit and I had neglected to introduce you to him, I would never hear the end of it."

The waiting room remained filled with people and more continued to file in through the entrance doors. Sand was still swirling about in front of the hospital and an Indian man swatted his stetson against his leg as he entered, spraying sand on a passing woman who grumbled to him in Navajo. The man looked away sheepishly.

John led Sam down another corridor off the waiting room area where a sign on the wall announced "Administrative Offices." Opening the first door they came to, John greeted the secretary and asked for Mr. Oliver.

She picked up the phone and pressed a buzzer. "Dr. Hartman is here with a visitor to see you."

She smiled at them. "Go right in."

Russell Oliver was a plump balding man with a cherubic countenance. Though he was approaching sixty, he was one of those people of indeterminate age, his corpulence giving him a younger rather than an older appearance. He had been in the Indian Health Service for almost twenty years and this was his last stop before retirement. John was well aware that he depended completely on his department heads to keep the hospital running smoothly. In return for their cooperation and their willingness to "watch the store" while he improved his golf game, they received the money appropriations necessary to buy whatever their departments needed.

He looked up from some papers he had put on top of the latest "Playboy" just before they entered and smiled at John.

"Mr. Oliver," said John, "this is Secretary of State Sam Spencer. Mr.Spencer, this is Mr. Oliver, Administrator of the Indian Medical Center."

Russel Oliver could not hide his astonishment and tripped over his chair as he sprang from it. "Mr. Secretary, this is indeed an honor," he gushed, extending his pudgy hand. "But we had no idea we were going to receive such a distinguished visitor."

"Well, actually, Mr. Oliver, I had no idea I would be here. I was driving to Albuquerque and brought a patient in."

"A patient?"

"Mr. Spencer found a sick Indian boy on the road and was kind enough to bring him here," explained John.

"Well, that was certainly good of you, sir. Please sit down—here, take this chair." He moved the leather chair from behind his desk toward Sam. "Is there anything we can do for you while you're here? We'd be very pleased to take you on a tour of our facility."

"Thank you, Mr. Oliver, that's very kind but I have to catch a flight out of Albuquerque at two and was wondering if I might call the airline to see if this sandstorm has caused any delay."

"Of course, of course." He passed a telephone directory and his phone to Sam. "Just press nine and you'll have an outside line."

Sam called American Airlines and was advised that the flight had been rescheduled for three-thirty. He handed the phone back to Oliver.

"Well, it looks like my flight is delayed a bit. It's fortunate, I suppose, because I probably couldn't have made it with that sand blowing out there."

"It shouldn't last much longer. The radio this morning said they expected the winds to die down by eleven or twelve," said Oliver reassuringly. "Would you like some coffee, Mr. Secretary?"

Sam declined and looked at John, hoping that the doctor would rescue him from Oliver's unctuous clutches. But the administrator was not to be put off.

"What brings you to our part of the country, Mr. Secretary? I'm sorry we couldn't offer you better weather—it's usually very pleasant this time of year."

"Yes, I know. That was why I decided to fly back to Washington from Albuquerque instead of Phoenix. I had hoped to see some of New Mexico again—it's been many years since I was here. My wife and I always loved this country."

The mention of Sam's wife was a sudden reminder to Russell Oliver. "I remember reading about the unfortunate death of your wife and son, Mr. Secretary. That was a good many years ago, of course, and I believe you were a U.S. attorney at the time."

"Yes, it was a long time ago," said Sam, surprised at his own mention of Kate and taken aback by the administrator's recall of the accident.

"Well, if you'll excuse me," said John, "I'd better get up to the ward and see how our patient is doing. And I'm sure Mr. Spencer is anxious to be on his way."

"I understand. It only grieves me, Mr. Secretary, to have had you here for such a short visit. We have an excellent staff here and we're quite proud of our institution, yes, quite proud. Well, I wish you a good journey and success in your coming negotiations."

"Thank you for being so gracious, Mr. Oliver, and for the use of your phone." They again shook hands and Sam noted with distaste that Oliver's hand was sweaty.

"Any time, any time. And please do come back to see us."

Sam felt relieved once they were out of the office. He looked at John and received a knowing smile in return. "As I said, he never would have forgiven me if he had found out you were here and I didn't take you to meet him."

"Well, if you don't mind I'd like to go up to the ward with you and see how the boy is doing. Now that I know the flight is delayed, there's no sense in driving through that sand again. If your administrator's forecast is correct I should be able to start out in about an hour or so."

As they rode the elevator to the ward, Sam thought about Oliver's reference to Kate's death. Reflecting upon it, he realized that a man in Oliver's position, a bureaucrat who had climbed each rung of the Indian Health Service's ladder and who obviously was no stranger to politics of one form or another, would remember something like that. It was no different, after all, at State. Every person there had as much of an interest, or perhaps more, in the personal life of government figures as in the operations of the department and its policies. Gossip was the order of the day and he had no reason to suppose it should be any different in the Health Service. He could imagine Oliver already making a series of calls to his acquaintances about his "distinguished" visitor. What most perplexed Sam was his own reference to Kate while talking to Oliver. He had not used the words "my wife and I" since her death. It was yet another symptom of the loosening of the reins he maintained on his emotions and he found it particularly disconcerting.

His thoughts were interrupted as they stepped off the elevator and were confronted by a small boy of about six. One side of his face was badly swollen and discolored. "Hello, Anthony," said John.

The boy smiled crookedly and held out a red checker piece.

"I can't right now, Anthony," he laughed, "but I promise to come back later for a game. All right?"

The boy nodded, apparently satisfied, and disappeared into a nearby room. The walls were covered with bright decorations and colorful pictures and there were small tables and chairs arranged to provide maximum floor space for the children. At least ten boys and girls were in the room, all absorbed in activities ranging from ring toss to painting.

"That's quite nice," said Sam, motioning toward the room.

"It's never easy to be a patient in a hospital, especially for a child. We try to make it as pleasant as possible."

"What happened to the little fellow's face?"

"Anthony? He had a run-in with a rattlesnake. Fortunately it happened not too far from here and he responded well to treatment."

"Not a run of the mill case for most hospitals, I imagine."

John laughed. "We get cases here that most hospitals in this country would consider very unusual."

The nurse at the desk was Navajo, as were the other personnel on the floor. She held out a chart as they approached. "Your new patient is in Room One, Dr. Hartman. He's had his first dose of Tetracycline. Elsie is with him and Dr. Moore is waiting to see you, too."

"Thanks, Andrea," he said, taking the chart from her and opening to the temperature record. "Hmmm. Temp's 104.8 and pulse 132. Still right up there."

They walked down to the room, which was small and contained only one bed. A "respiratory precautions" sign was on the door and they put on gowns and masks before entering. Bill Moore stood in front of one wall holding X-Ray films up to a view box and indicating something to the young Indian nurse at his side.

"Oh, hi, John," he called. "Hello, Mr. Spencer. Well, our young friend has a diffuse pneumonitis in both lungs, including the apices. Harvey Adams checked the films, too, and he agrees. Lee called from the lab and WBC's are 15,000 with 72 segs, 12 stabs. Hemoglobin and crit are low normal."

John looked at the X-Rays and nodded. "Those mediastinal nodes are really enlarged."

They were interrupted by a gasping sound from the bed, followed by a fit of coughing. The child struggled to get his breath as sputum ran down his chin staining the white sheet red.

"Elsie, let's get some additional cultures on that sputum including acid-fast. Call respiratory therapy, too, about hooking up some O2. And let's tape on a urine bag. If he doesn't have some output pretty soon I'll put a catheter in."

As she left the room, Bill Moore shook his head. "This kid's really in bad shape, John. He's been getting more restless and having more difficulty breathing."

"We'll get a few more doses of antibiotics into him and if he doesn't respond by tonight, we'll have to consider a chopper evac to Albuquerque in the morning."

"I wonder what the organism is," mused Bill Moore. "I don't believe it's TB."

"I don't either," agreed John. "We'll just have to see if we grow something from the sputum or blood. But I agree that it's weird. The sputum is like red syrup."

"We sure haven't had pulmonary cases on Medicine to compare with this. You guys have all the luck. And I don't mind keeping it that way."

Sam stood in the background while the two men discussed the case. How odd, how inconceivable, he thought, to find himself in an Indian hospital. He had lived in the Southwest long enough to realize the plight of the Indians and yet had never felt the desire to become involved in their problems. They had been merely a sometimes colorful, sometimes drab, but more often invisible, backdrop to his life. Kate and Jeff hadn't shared his disinterest and ultimately it had cost them their lives.

His mother-in-law, of course, had been a well-known advocate of Native American causes as well as a consulting attorney for the Navajo Tribal Council. Sam had respected her dedication to her work but was often inclined to think of her as a quixotic idealist. Once he had left Flagstaff, shortly after Kate's death, he had never thought of the Indians or their problems, or for that matter, of Julia and her work. Anything, he believed, that reminded him of the pain he had experienced was best forgotten—and in Washington there were no Indians to stir up memories.

In spite of these feelings, he was able to appreciate the efforts of these young Anglo doctors working in an Indian hospital in a nondescript town that probably felt toward them only a guarded hostility, or at best, indifference. He thought of the reactions of the two Anglos on the road and remembered that the Indians were the "blacks" of the Southwest.

Something else had dawned on him, too. The staff of the hospital appeared to be predominantly Indian—he had seen Indian nurses and Indian secretaries and that meant a change had occurred even in the educational process. When he had lived in the southwest, few Anglos thought there was any justification for teaching Indians. "Uneducable" was the word he had often heard from teachers.

"Incapable of even learning English." And just the day before he had even noticed a small article in the Flagstaff paper about a proposed medical school for Native Americans.

He wondered how the average Anglo would react to the idea of a Navajo doctor and imagined the discomfort it was likely to cause. His musings were interrupted suddenly by a commotion in the corridor.

"Elsie, better see what's happening out there," said John Hartman.

The nurse started for the door but was swept back and almost knocked off her feet by the tumultuous entrance of a large Navajo woman wearing traditional dress. A magnificent squash-blossom necklace of silver and turquoise covered the bodice of her velveteen blouse. Two other nurses were dragged into the room as they held on to the woman in a vain attempt to restrain her. Everyone was yelling in Navajo and it was impossible to know what was happening until John stepped in front of her and raised his hand.

"Let her go," he commanded softly to the two nurses and they released their grip on her arms. The woman turned and said something to each of them. There was no mistaking her anger and they shrunk back, half expecting her to strike out at them.

"What's this all about?" asked John.

"She says we're holding her grandson here," answered one of the nurses. "The description she gives is of the boy who was admitted a little while ago. We told her we would have you come out to see her but she wouldn't wait."

In the meantime, the woman had spotted the boy in the bed. She pushed past John and walked over to see him, then let out a piercing wail. Turning toward John, she began shouting at him in Navajo.

"Does she speak any English?" John asked the nurses. They shook their heads. "Ask her if that is her grandson."

"It is," replied Elsie. "She's yelling that you have no right to keep him here in the hospital.."

"Elsie, tell her the boy is very sick in his lungs and that without treatment he'll die. Tell her we're going to try to save him but that if our medicine isn't strong enough we'll have to send him to Albuquerque."

The woman had now turned away from them and was speaking in a barely audible whisper to the boy, who remained unresponsive. She placed her hand on his head and stroked his hair.

Elsie began talking to her softly and at first they thought she hadn't heard since she did not turn around. But then she spoke with her back to them and although much of her anger appeared to have subsided, her voice remained harsh.

"She says she is taking the boy with her. She wants to take him to her doctor and to the Singer. She says they will cure him."

John Hartman remained calm. "Elsie, what's her name and what's the boy called?"

Elsie asked the question.

"She is Mary Begay. The boy is Joseph Williams."

"Tell her that I believe in the medicine of the Singer, too, but that I'd like to try my medicine first. In the meantime, she can make plans for the Sing. When the boy is strong enough to leave here we'll tell her and then the Sing can be held."

This information was relayed to Mary Begay, who turned to look at John and then, shaking her head, gave her reply to Elsie.

"She says the boy is dying and the only chance to save him now is with the medicine of her people."

"Ask her how long the boy has been sick."

"She thinks for about two or three days. He had a fever and some vomiting. She gave him some herbs yesterday."

"Tell her we've taken pictures of the boy's lungs. That there is a bad sickness in there and that he must have strong medicine to save his life. If she takes him out of the hospital, he'll surely die."

Sam watched the exchange in amazement. I'd like to have him as a negotiator, he thought. John Hartman never lost his patience. Over and over again he repeated his words in an effort to convince the woman. It had become a battle of wills. Although the woman's face now revealed a rugged obstinacy, Sam thought that under different circumstances it would have shown a soft, gentle quality. The crow's feet at the corners of her eyes and the faint wrinkles around her lips appeared to be those associated with a face that smiled often. But there was no smiling now. The woman's dark eyes remained hard and her lips, when she was not speaking, were drawn into a firm line.

John sighed and looked at Bill Moore. "There's nothing else we can do, Bill. She insists on taking him out."

"Do you think it would help if we brought Tom up to talk to her?"

He shook his head. "No social worker will convince her, I'm afraid. Not even Tom."

The woman knew she had won and without saying anything else she pointed at the IV. After John had removed the needle from the child's arm, she wrapped the boy in the blanket from the bed and lifted him into her strong arms as if he were only an infant.

She walked past them and turned at the door to face John. There was a moment of silence and they could hear only the stertorous, forced breathing of the child. She said a final few words and then disappeared.

Everyone stared at the spot where only seconds earlier Mary Begay had stood holding Joseph Williams in her arms. The boy had suddenly been removed from their lives, from any chance he had to survive, and left behind were the unused intravenous solution and the used IV tubing. With their efforts thwarted, each of the doctors and nurses lapsed into a silence that was indicative of the frustration felt. It was only Sam Spencer, the one non-medical person in the room, who, overwhelmed by what had just occurred, felt obliged to express what everyone inwardly felt. "Is that it then? She's going to take that boy out of the hospital to his death and there's nothing anyone can do?"

His question remained unanswered but served to shatter the state of inanimation that pervaded the room.

"What did she say when she left, Elsie?" asked John.

"She said she would return the blanket."

"Is that all?"

Elsie lowered her eyes. In the old days, when spoken to, a Navajo would never look into the eyes of the speaker. Only the moving lips were watched. Elsie was far removed from many of the old customs and looked away from Doctor Hartman only because of the difficulty of trying to express in a way any white man could understand what Mary Begay had meant. And since it was totally contrary to the nature of a Navajo to lie, she could certainly not bear to confront his questioning look.

"She said 'thank you'."

"Well," sighed Bill Moore, "another chance for a therapeutic triumph shot to hell."

John looked at him with a trace of a smile on his lips. "How do you know?"

"How do I know what? Oh, come on, John, I know you're into this Indian ritualistic healing and we all know there's a definite psychological benefit, but this kid was moribund. I'm no pediatrician but I know a kid dying of pneumonia when I see one."

Elsie and the other nurses had begun removing the equipment from the room while Andrea stripped the sheet and pillow case from the bed. They evinced no interest in the conversation taking place between the two physicians.

"Look, Bill," argued John, "suppose we had treated the boy and he had died, which was not unlikely, you know. How would Mary Begay have felt then knowing that the traditional medicine of her people had never had its chance?"

Bill Moore was unable to disguise his exasperation. "John, I respect you and I respect their beliefs, but I'm too much of a pragmatist to accept what sounds like bullshit. The only chance that kid had was right here in this room—and you know it!"

"I don't really disagree with you, Bill. Of course the boy should have remained here. I'm only trying to say that modern science doesn't have the answers to everything—you know that. Customs, mores, beliefs, the legacy of centuries of a more ancient civilization than our own are equally important."

"My God, protect me from mystics!" His irritation evident, Bill Moore walked out of the room, not stopping to take leave of the people remaining. Andrea appeared to have ignored the altercation and simply removed the soiled linen from the room without saying a word.

Sam, more perplexed than ever, could only ask helplessly, "But why did you let that woman take the boy in the first place? It was her grandson, not her son. Why didn't you demand that the boy's mother come?"

"The woman was head of her clan. She had the right to make the decision."

Sam shook his head. "It's simply too much to comprehend. This is twentieth century America, not some primitive civilization in a third-world backwater."

John laughed. "Words like primitive and civilization are only relative, you know. Can I get you some coffee?"

Sam turned to look out of the window. Columns of sand still swirled from the flat expanse of land that stretched to the south and most of the homes of Gallup were visible one moment, then obliterated the next under a fresh assault of wind-driven sand.

"Might as well—it's still miserable out there. I'm afraid that if it doesn't subside pretty soon I'll have to take my chances and keep driving. I can't afford to miss my flight."

"I'm surprised really that you're using commercial transportation and traveling without any protection. That's not standard procedure, is it?"

Being reminded of his impulsive action irked Sam Spencer. "No, it isn't," he replied defensively, "but I was in Arizona for a funeral—a family affair—and wanting privacy, it was my choice to travel this way."

John led Sam down the Pediatrics corridor to a small staff lounge. It was empty except for a round table with three chairs and a coffee maker. John poured two cups and placed them on the table.

"We have some creamer and sugar, if you'd like."

"Thanks," said Sam, "black will be fine. You know, a few things puzzle me. Actually, more than a few but the ones that come to mind are, first of all, how did that Begay woman know that the boy was in the hospital?"

"That's really not too surprising," smiled John. "I'm sure you were seen by at least a dozen Indians when you put the boy in your car to bring him here. One of them must have gotten word to Mary Begay."

"It does surprise me that they even bothered to do that. Not one of them offered to help me—and most of them were in no condition to anyway."

"Don't forget, Mr. Spencer, you're an Anglo—and even when an Anglo's motives appear to be good, the Indians have learned through sad experience that things are not always what they seem to be. As far as the drinking goes, well, that's one of our biggest social and health problems. Cirrhosis of the liver is the fourth biggest killer of the Indians. The Anglos found out long ago that alcohol was more effective—and less open to criticism—than shooting to subdue the Indians. Thousands of them are crippled now by the disease. Do you know that we have eighteen and nineteen year olds with cirrhosis? Just last week we lost a sixteen year old boy with acute alcohol intoxication.

"We also have a lot of trauma cases from drinking. After getting wiped out in Gallup on booze, some of the Indians try to drive back to the reservation. The accidents are really horrible. In fact, accidents of one kind or another are the leading killer of Indians. One out of every five Indian deaths is caused by an accident."

For a moment, Sam's thoughts darted to Kate and Jeff. They, too, had died in a flaming car wreck on the way to an Indian festival. He struggled now to suppress the perverse notion of retribution that flitted through his mind.

"What did the woman mean about wanting to take the boy to her doctor and to the Singer?" he asked.

"By the doctor she probably meant the hand trembler. Once he makes the diagnosis the Sing will be arranged. And that's where the Singer comes in."

"You've lost me on all this," said Sam. "I haven't any idea what a hand trembler or Sing or Singer is."

"Where to begin?" said John. "I didn't know any of this either when I came here three years ago." He paused, grappling with the ideas he was trying to put into words. "To a Navajo, the most important thing is to keep his life in harmony with the universe—and with things supernatural. Illness to a Navajo means that that harmony has been disrupted. When we talk about curing or healing, to a Navajo that means restoring harmony. Maybe balance is a better word. And actually, all aspects of Navajo life—the social, the religious, the medical—are aimed at restoring this harmony.

"How does the hand trembler come into this?" asked Sam.

"The hand trembler is their equivalent of a family physician. He's the diagnostician. It's his job to diagnose the cause of the illness and he doesn't do it by anything he's learned, like one of our doctors would. He does it by his mystical gifts. Naturally, a hand trembler's diagnosis will bear no resemblance whatever to the diagnosis one of our doctors would make. They don't think in the same terms. For example, we diagnosed that boy as having pneumonia. The hand trembler may diagnose a spell cast by white people or a violation of some taboo. Then once he makes his diagnosis by using his special powers, he has to find the correct Sing. That's the particular ceremonial that will bring about the cure."

"And that brings us to the Singer?" asked Sam.

John nodded. "Exactly. We'd think of the Singer as a medicine man but he's much more than that. He's the Navajo high priest and the only one who can cure illness. And that doesn't mean he treats the symptoms or does what an Anglo doctor does. Once again, his job is to restore the patient to harmony and to do that he uses a very intricate and involved ceremony. A Singer has to train for his work with an established Singer and he has to learn hundreds of songs and chants. They have to be word-perfect and even sung with the right intonation. If he makes a mistake more evil may occur. Also, he has to know all the legends and herbs and fetishes and how to make sand paintings—all the different things that go into the ceremony. It takes years of training and even though there are about thirty-five major ceremonial sings, most Singers only know two or three of them. That's why the correct Singer has to be found for a particular illness. A Sing may take just a day or it can go on for more than a week, day and night. It's an expensive proposition for a Navajo family. It can cost them months of income."

"If the Navajos still believe in this traditional medicine," asked Sam, "and I assume most of them still do, then why do they come to this hospital and permit themselves to be treated by white doctors?"

John laughed. "The Navajo, you know, is really a pragmatist. When it comes to treating symptoms, like pain for instance, he'll resort to whatever makes the pain go away. He may see a herbalist or an Anglo doctor or even a faith healer. They're all lumped in the same basket. Some of the new doctors arriving here are shocked to learn that even after performing a life-saving surgery or setting a fracture, they're still low man on the totem pole in the healing hierarchy, no better than a Navajo herb dispenser. But, again, that's because of the basic concept of health to a Navajo. Restoring harmony is the name of the game—that's what Singers do and that's what's most important.

"Here's an example. One of our anesthetists, a former psychiatric social worker in Las Cruces, mind you, had her car break down on a deserted road about ten miles from here. This happened only about two weeks ago. She went walking for help and stumbled into a hole which proved to be an open grave. Within a day or two she had seen one of the local Singers and he did the Blessingway chant for her so that once again she might "walk in beauty." John indicated the quotation marks with his index fingers.

Sam watched John's face as he spoke. He knew that Hartman was young, not more than thirty-three or four. His face had a boyish quality and the prominent gap between his two front teeth only accentuated his youthful appearance. His hair was dark brown and of shirt collar length. But his eyes, a true grey not speckled with any other color, held Sam fast when he spoke. It was the intensity of that gaze and his obvious intelligence that led Sam to realize very quickly that he possessed a wisdom beyond his years.

"Another thing that gives Anglo doctors trouble," continued John, "is the Navajo thought process. If that boy, for example, had some minor problem the mother, if she was here, would have consented for us to treat him. But for a major illness the whole family will get together to discuss things and it's ultimately the grandmother, as head of the extended family, who makes the decision.

"Also, it's not uncommon for a Navajo to request a Sing before permitting us to give treatment. Sometimes I think they're just testing us to see how understanding we are about their traditions."

"You certainly seem quite sympathetic to their traditions," said Sam.

"Well, I look at it this way. I think one of the biggest mistakes we whites make, and not only here in Navajoland, is to assume that the Anglo way, because it's modern and technologically superior, is the right way. The Anglo tries to strip away the culture of the Indian, or any other aboriginal people, because it's primitive and unintelligible, and to an Anglo's way of thinking that means bad. Just think what's been done to Indians in the name of Anglo religion, Anglo science, Anglo culture.

"I believe white doctors should collaborate with the Navajo Singers. After all, if we have the patient's best interest at heart, then we have to realize that's what will make the patient and his family feel better. I often permit families to take their children home for Sings."

"Well, much of what you say is true, of course," replied Sam, "but it still doesn't justify that woman pulling her grandson out of the hospital when he's critically ill and it will probably lead to his death. I'm afraid I have to agree with Dr. Moore on that."

"I can understand the frustration that arouses in an Anglo and that's why Bill was so upset, of course. And although my rational, scientific self says of course it was the wrong thing to do and it's robbing that boy of the only real chance he had to survive, another part of me says just a minute now—what arrogance to think that the Anglo way is necessarily the right way." He smiled at the thoughtful expression on Sam's face. "Believe me, I go round and round with this in my own mind. There's no easy answer."

Sam shook his head. "I admit it's all very complex and that I've never looked at things in that way."

"I didn't mean for this to turn into a lecture," said John. "I gather you've spent time in this area?"

"Yes, I used to live in Flagstaff and I've travelled in New Mexico quite a bit. But that was years ago. I only went back to Arizona yesterday for the funeral of my wife's mother."

"I'm sorry," said John.

"Well, we'd been out of contact for years—since my wife was killed. My mother-in-law was quite a woman. She was a lawyer, very active in Indian causes. You and she would have hit it off very well."

Sam's words aroused John Hartman's own troubled memories. He stood up and refilled their coffee cups. "I noticed," he said, attempting to choose his words carefully, "that you were a bit upset in Mr. Oliver's office when he mentioned your wife and son. I'm afraid our administrator's sensibilities are a bit blunted at times."

"Oh, you don't have to apologize for him. I suppose he was just trying to let me know that he has an interest in my life. We have a lot of Russell Olivers at State."

They sat in silence for a few moments listening to the sand and dust being hurled against the window by blasts of wind. Sam stared moodily into space, turning his cup in his fingers. "My wife and son were killed ten years ago outside of Flagstaff," he said slowly. "They were driving to an Indian dance festival. There was some light rain and they either skidded or were forced off the road by another car. They rolled over several times and were apparently killed instantly. Jeff was ten at the time." He paused, self-conscious about the tremor in his voice, and cleared his throat. "Kate was very interested in Indian culture. Her mother used to talk to her for hours about tribal legends and her enthusiasm rubbed off on Jeff. It's absurd, I know, but I suppose that in some way I blame the Indians for their deaths.

I've tried not to think about any of it for these last ten years—not about Kate or Jeff or Indians or the Southwest. It surprised me actually that I came back for the funeral when I learned of my mother-in-law's death. Maybe I subconsciously thought it was time to confront the past again. Kate and I used to do quite a bit of camping here on vacations. The more rugged the country was the more we loved it. Once I'd made the decision to return to Flagstaff for the funeral it was inevitable, I suppose, that I decide to drive through the country we'd shared so happily." He fumbled now for his pipe and, embarrassed by his candor, stared at the window. "All this dust blowing about may be an indication that when things are buried it's best to leave them that way."

"You never remarried?" asked John.

Sam shook his head. "No, my work became my wife and mistress. I suppose I'd be considered successful by most people."

"And by yourself?"

Sam shrugged. "That's enough about me. Are you married?"

"No. I guess you could say I'm both divorced and a widower." And then, just as Sam Spencer had opened up to him, John found himself telling Sam about Janet and Valentina and Gabriella. It was the first time he had talked to anyone about them since the evening of the killings, when he had talked to Detective Keats. He blinked away the tears that threatened to come. "So, it looks like you and I have the unfortunate distinction of having known tragedy in our lives."

Sam cleared his throat. "I take it you haven't married again?"

John shook his head. "It's just as well, you know. There aren't many people who would voluntarily live in Gallup. If you're an outsider here—and that means not belonging to the old trading families—you're excluded from what social life there is. But there are compensations apart from the satisfaction of the work. The country is desolate and arid, but as you found out, it's beautiful in its own way. I'm a photography buff and also dabble in watercolors so esthetically I find it offers me quite a bit. And when I feel the need to get to the big city, which really isn't too often, I go to Albuquerque or Santa Fe. The longer I'm here, too, my need to be an amateur sociologist and anthropologist is fulfilled by the Navajo and Hopi cultures—I do find them fascinating."

Sam smiled. "Have you tried to learn to speak Navajo? It sounds unlike anything I've ever heard."

"Except for a few words, I'm afraid not. It's an unwritten language and very complex—I've yet to meet an Anglo, except for our social worker here and he's unusual, who really speaks Navajo. That's true even of Anglos who have lived on the reservation for years. You probably know that during the Second World War Navajos were used to send communications—the enemy could never decipher those messages."

Sam stood up now and walked to the window. The winds appeared to be dying down and it was possible to see more of the town and surrounding desert. He watched a train rumbling slowly along its track, heading west to Arizona. Boxcar followed boxcar in what seemed an unending succession.

"Well," sighed Sam, "it's time for me to get going if I'm to make my flight. It's been a pleasure to meet you and quite an educational experience. If you ever do find out anything about that Indian boy, Joseph, I hope you'll drop me a line."

"I'll be sure to do that," said John, leading him to the elevator, where Sam insisted it wasn't necessary for John to accompany him to the lobby. They shook hands warmly.

"I hope you have a pleasant trip back to civilization," said John, using his fingers to put quotation marks around civilization.

"I often wonder about that word myself," said Sam.

"Good luck in the peace talks," called John. Sam waved as the elevator door closed.

There goes a troubled man, said John to himself. Well, I guess that makes two of us. He returned to the ward and went to look for Anthony. The boy sat in the playroom at the little table, the checkerboard set up in front of him, and smiled as John entered.

CHAPTER 3 _____

THE BATTERED AND SCRAPED PICKUP TRUCK, ITS blue body fifteen years old and looking worse than the hulks found in automobile graveyards, strained and bounced down a tortuous rock-filled path that was designated as a road on a map of the Navajo reservation. It was no worse a road than most of those found on the reservation and better than some.

The sun was high now in the sky and only an occasional dust cloud swirled about them as the winds subsided. The worst of the sandstorm was past here on the higher plateau north of Gallup and the warmth of the sun filled the cab of the pickup.

Hosteen Williams, the driver, used both the sun visor and the brim of his stetson to shield his eyes from the glare. His muscular arms, bared by flannel sleeves rolled up above the elbows, controlled the wheel. It was necessary for him to keep a firm grip at all times as the ruts and stones of the road threatened to tear the wheel from his hands at any moment.

The concentration was apparent on his broad, weather-lined face. His small eyes were made to appear even smaller by his high cheekbones and the wire-rimmed spectacles he wore. What could be seen of his hair from beneath the stetson was grey and cut short. Hosteen was fifty years old, the second oldest of Mary Begay's eleven children, and like most of his brothers and sisters was a sheep herder. Except for a two year stint in the Army served at Fort Sill, Oklahoma, he had spent his entire life on the reservation. He had been a widower for many years and his three children were all gone now. He understood their rejection of the harsh life of Navajoland but their leaving the reservation had hurt him nevertheless. Their letters now arrived from the white man's cities of Chicago, Tulsa and Boise and sometimes, as he read of their new lives, he wondered if they were really his children and still Navajos at all. His two sons and daughter were aware of the rift that had grown between them and their father over the years and whereas they had tried at first to make regular visits back to the reservation, they now contented themselves with occasional letters that contained whatever money they could spare.

Next to him sat his mother, Mary Begay, and cradled in her arms was her grandson and his nephew, Joseph Williams. The boy was still unconscious and the only sound in the cab was that of his labored breathing and intermittent coughing. Mary held the boy's head turned to her breast to keep the sun from his face and used a corner of her shawl to wipe off the red-stained mucus that dribbled from his lips.

Her mouth was firmly set and, like her son, she stared directly ahead at the road, which ran across an arid, flat plain, and then later curved and twisted through more rugged mesaland perched on the walls of boulder-littered canyons. She felt the heat emanating from the boy's body but if she experienced concern for his condition, her face did not betray it.

Hosteen Williams had been driving for almost an hour since leaving the hospital in Gallup. His eyes were fixed now on a point just beyond a butte-shaped rock to the west. At first glance there was nothing visible other than the brown and grey pastel colors of the rocks and small clumps of mezquite and ocotillo. There was some movement among the vegetation and a few sheep appeared, followed by a hairless brown mongrel that stared impassively at the truck bouncing along in its direction.

It was not until they had passed the largest rocks that the hogan became visible, blending into the land and seemingly a direct outgrowth of it.

The low dome-shaped structure was made of logs and mud covered with earth and had a central smoke-hole in the roof. It had no windows and the only ventilation for the dwelling was provided by the cracks around the one door leading into it and by the smoke-hole. The doorway faced to the east so the inhabitant could see the dawn. To the side of the hogan was a gasoline drum for water storage and beyond that one could see a stack of firewood tied in teepee fashion.

Except for sheep and the dog, which now wagged its tail lazily, there was no sign of life as the pickup truck approached.

Hosteen guided the vehicle almost to the door of the hogan and turned off the engine. The silence of the mesas immediately surrounded them and they could hear only the harsh breathing of Joseph Williams.

The door of the hogan suddenly opened and a gaunt Navajo dressed in faded denims appeared. He was taller than most Indians and wore no hat. His hair hung shoulder length, accentuating the lean, drawn appearance of his face. His sharp aquiline nose and sunken cheeks gave him the fevered look of a Biblical ascetic.

Harvey Running Bear was born in this same hogan fifty years ago. His mother had died when he was still young and his father was killed shortly after that when he fell asleep drunk on the Santa Fe tracks. His brother and sisters had gradually drifted away but Harvey remained and still lived in the hogan. When he was younger he had worked for short periods of time on Anglo ranches off the reservation but inevitably his longing for the solitude of the mesas brought him back to his ancestral home. He had taken a wife during one of his sojourns away from Dinetah, Old Navajo Land, and brought her home with him to his hogan. Bright Sparrow was an Apache, no more than fifteen when she went to live with Running Bear. One year later, she bled her life away on the earth floor of the hogan in a vain attempt to bear her child. The baby, too, was dead by the time Harvey could get her into Gallup.

For a long time no one would visit the "chindee hogan," the place where death had occurred. Later the word got out that Bright Sparrow had actually breathed her last on the trip into Gallup. That was why Running Bear had not abandoned his hogan and built a new one to the east.

He had never married again and shortly after his wife's death, Harvey Running Bear had had a mystical experience. He was visited one star-filled night by the Spirit of the Gila Monster. For many weeks after that visitation Harvey had been sick, burning with fever, but when the malady passed, Harvey knew that he had "the gift." From that time on he had been a hand trembler.

The hogans and woodframe or adobe cracker-box houses of Dinetah were miles apart. Harvey's nearest neighbor was three miles to the west across canyons and unpaved roads. Nevertheless, word of Harvey's abilities with divination had spread and he was now recognized as the most famous hand trembler in the region. His diagnoses were invariably correct and a necessary prelude to the eventual restoration of harmony by the Singer.

Hosteen stepped down from the truck and clasped Harvey's hand. They remained like that for several seconds, their hands gently touching, neither man speaking. They had not seen one another for many months.

At last Hosteen spoke, indicating the truck as he did so. Harvey glanced momentarily at Mary Begay and nodded. Hosteen then went to the other side of the cab and took the boy from Mary's arms. Mary descended and they both followed Running Bear into the hogan.

The one room was immersed in darkness except for the light that filtered in around the smoke hole and through the door cracks. It was also at least twenty degrees cooler than outside in the noonday sun. Harvey lit a kerosene lamp that rested upon a large flat rock. The hogan was completely devoid of furniture and the shadows of the people danced eerily upon the mud walls.

Harvey's bed was a sheepskin stretched out on the dirt floor next to the gasoline drum stove in the center of the hogan. A makeshift chimney rose from the stove to the smoke hole. The stove was still faintly warm from the cooking of breakfast hours before. Also near the stove on the pounded dirt floor was a section of oilcloth, upon which Harvey ate his meals.

There were few objects in the hogan. Some pots, pans, and utensils occupied one corner and next to them were staple items—flour, salt, and pepper. In another corner an old shotgun rested against the wall. Two pegs formed from heavy branches protruded from the wooden door and a blanket and pair of pants hung from these.

Running Bear took the boy's limp body from Hosteen and placed him on the sheepskin. He looked intently at Joseph Williams and grunted.

"You can undress him," he said to Mary. "I'll go for water while you gather some firewood," he instructed Hosteen.

"I didn't see your truck," said Hosteen as the two men left the hogan. "I wasn't sure you were here."

"Charlie Bigwater came over early this morning to borrow it. His wife has some rugs for the trader."

The two men stood in silence and watched a hawk circling lazily above them. Running Bear nodded as if in answer to an unspoken question only he had heard. "The boy is very sick, Hosteen. The spirits are killing his body."

"Do you think you can find the cause?"

"I'll try. After you get the wood why don't you ride over to Homer Red Arrow in Tohatchi. Tell him we need some good medicine for the boy to make him feel better until the Sing is held. And while you're there you can talk to Sam Begay about arranging the Sing. How soon do you think you can make preparations for it?"

Hosteen thought for several minutes without saying anything. This was not a matter to be taken lightly. There were people to invite, food had to be prepared and payment had to be arranged. A sand painting also needed to be done and time had to be allowed for this. But he knew that with Joseph Williams so ill, he could not wait very long.

"I think we can be ready by tomorrow," he mumbled almost to himself. "If Sam is willing."

Running Bear nodded. "Good," he said simply and then walked to the water tank.

Hosteen, in the meantime, gathered up some pieces of wood from the stack beyond the water drum and carried them to the hogan. He found Mary sitting on the floor watching Joseph. She did not look up when he came in. The boy's thin body was now completely naked. His breathing had worsened, becoming more irregular with a gurgling sound that seemed to arise from deep within his chest, and his entire body trembled with the effort to get air into his lungs.

Hosteen could readily see that despite the overwhelming problems involved in arranging a Sing on such short notice, his judgement had been correct. Joseph Williams was losing in his battle with the evil spirits and only the immediate intervention of the power of the Singer could help the boy now. He informed his mother that he was heading over to Tohatchi to see the herbalist and make arrangements for the Sing.

She looked up at him. "It will have to be done very soon. Can you get word to everyone?"

He nodded, inwardly relieved that his mother concurred in the need for haste.

"I will stay here then," she said, sighing almost imperceptibly.

Hosteen placed the wood by the stove and glancing once more at his nephew left the hogan. Running Bear approached with a can of water and the two men nodded as they passed each other. There was nothing left to say and Hosteen swung his body into the driver's seat of the truck. As he drove away he could see the first few wisps of smoke coming from the roof of the hogan.

Inside, Running Bear had begun his preparations for the ceremony. The fire was going in the stove and he and Mary washed the boy's fevered body, cupping the water in their hands and letting it trickle over him.

Running Bear then went to a crevice in one wall of the hogan and withdrew a small leather pouch. From this, he took a powdery substance and then squatted next to Joseph Williams. Mary watched as he rubbed sacred corn pollen on the boy's body, first on his feet and legs, then his hands and chest, always working from right to left. He then asked Mary to place the boy in a sitting position and finished spreading the pollen on Joseph's back and on the top of his head. As Mary let the boy sink again into a reclining position, Running Bear rubbed the remainder of the pollen on his own right arm, beginning at the vein in the inside of the elbow and continuing to the tips of his fingers.

He shifted now into a kneeling position and began to pray. His lips barely moved as he intoned the Navajo chants to the Gila Monster. Because Harvey had the spirit of the Gila Monster within him he asked the spirit to tell him what was wrong with the sick boy, offering shells and turquoise in return. After four repetitions of the prayers, Running Bear invoked the Gila Monster with songs, listening at the same time with his right arm extended.

Mary Begay could see a slight tremor in the outstretched fingers and then suddenly the entire arm and hand began to shake violently. Running Bear's concentration was so intense that he seemed unaware of the movements of his extremity. He appeared only to be listening to an unheard voice.

The shaking of his hand and arm subsided, only to begin again moments later. This sequence of events continued until his arm abruptly fell to his side and he appeared to waken from a trance.

Once again the Gila Monster had shown its acceptance of him and he had been able to determine the cause of the patient's illness. He stood up, stretched, and, indicating a pot near the stove, asked Mary to heat up the coffee that remained from the morning.

Mary did not ask what Running Bear had learned. In his own time, she knew, he would tell her.

He puttered around in one corner of the hogan and came up with two cups. These he handed to Mary and she poured the steaming black coffee for them. They drank in silence, their attention focused on Joseph Williams's struggle to breathe.

"The evil winds have brought this sickness to the boy. He will need the Windways chant."

Those were the only words he was to utter to Mary for the remainder of the afternoon. Shortly after he had finished his coffee, he picked up the old shotgun, found a few shells in a small crack in the hogan wall, and left the dwelling.

Mary in the meantime dressed Joseph Williams and tried to get him to drink some of the water that remained in the can. At intervals throughout the afternoon, she carefully poured small amounts between his parched lips but more often than not the boy would begin to cough, spitting out the liquid along with globs of blood-flecked mucus.

The small amount of light filtering through the cracks into the hogan began to fade as the hours passed. It was shortly before nightfall when Running Bear reappeared. In one hand he held the carcass of a jackrabbit, already skinned. He grunted with satisfaction as he replaced the shotgun in its corner of the room and laid the rabbit on the flat rock next to the kerosene lamp. Running Bear's moving form threw grotesque shadows on the walls. The light outside had completely disappeared now and they depended entirely on the lamp.

In contrast to the cold evening air of the desert outside, the interior of the hogan was warm enough from the fire that still burned in the stove to cause beads of perspiration to appear on Mary Begay's forehead.

Running Bear checked the supply of wood and went out to get more to last through the evening. While he was gone, Mary heard the sound of the approaching pickup truck. Moments later, Running Bear entered with the wood and behind him was Hosteen. They all squatted now around the stove as Harvey fed some more branches to the fire. The light of the flames danced on their faces as Hosteen spoke.

"I got the medicine from Homer Red Arrow," he said, producing from his shirt pocket two small packets of folded newspaper. Each contained herbs and he pointed out that Red Arrow had indicated the one looking like tea leaves was to be used first after boiling it for at least a half hour. Once the boy had drunk that, the second, made up of larger dark green leaves, was to be given, again after boiling, but for a shorter time.

Mary said she would like to begin to boil the water and Running Bear handed her the water can and a pot.

"I also saw Sam Begay," continued Hosteen. "He says he will begin the preparations for the Sing tonight providing it is the Windways or the Shooting chant. I'll have to go back to Tohatchi later to let him know."

"It is Windways," said Running Bear. "The boy is afflicted with the evil winds."

Hosteen's face looked relieved. He knew that Running Bear must have suspected it even before the hand trembling or he would not have sent him to Sam Begay. Of course, if Running Bear's assumptions had proven wrong, it would have been necessary to see a different Singer since Sam Begay knew only the Windways and Shooting chants.

"I have spoken also to some of our family," said Hosteen, "and they will get word to the others. They will try to reach Frank and Lilly in Shiprock. We are to meet at Sam Begay's hogan tomorrow at dawn. I have already arranged with everyone about the food. We are to bring Sam Begay twenty sheep and five hundred dollars. The Sing is expected to last for three nights."

Mary nodded silently. The price was high but would bring great prestige to the family. Although the boy's parents both worked at the electronics plant in Shiprock, Mary knew that the whole family would have to help them get the money together. She herself would have to pawn some of her silver and turquoise jewelry. Unconsciously, she glanced at the heavy silver bracelet on her wrist. The inlays of turquoise reflected the light from the fire. This was her bank account and she would pawn it, along with her rings if necessary, at the trading post.

The sound of the water boiling interrupted her thoughts. She took the first packet given to Hosteen by the herbalist and emptied the finely shredded leaves into the water.

Running Bear suddenly looked up from his spot near the stove. "Charlie Bigwater is coming," he said. Hosteen and Mary listened but could hear nothing. After a full minute had gone by they could hear the sound of a vehicle approaching. They were not surprised that Harvey Running Bear had known of its approach long before they had. They knew that the spirit of the Gila Monster told him many things.

A pickup truck pulled up outside the hogan and they heard the doors slam. Harvey went outside and returned leading an Indian couple that provided a strange contrast. The man was extremely tall, at least six-four, while the woman behind him was no more than five feet high.

Charlie Bigwater's appearance could only be called impressive. His muscular chest and shoulders threatened to burst from the light windbreaker he wore. His mother, a full-blooded Navajo, had married an Anglo lumberman, a Swede, and Charlie had spent his childhood around the lumber camps of Oregon. By the time he was fourteen he was felling trees as well as any of the men but his career came to an end two years after that when his father was crushed to death in a log jam on the Clackamas River.

His mother returned to the reservation and Charlie, who had taken her name, became a sheepherder. Despite the long braids he wore, his sharp features and light hair were unmistakable evidence of his mixed blood. To the Navajos, however, this was unimportant. Tribal customs did not prevent a Navajo from marrying into another tribe or race and the offspring of such a marriage were treated the same as full-bloods.

Charlie Bigwater's wife, Betsy Lee, was one of the best known rug weavers on the reservation. Her wood frame loom was set up near her hogan and every step in the making of the rugs, from the shearing and washing of the wool to the designs formulated in her mind, was done by her alone. Some of her designs were exhibited in the Navajo Guild's museum in Window Rock.

She was a petite woman with a pixie-like quality, unusual in a Navajo past thirty. Despite her weaving ability she wore a cheap factory-made blanket over her shoulders, giving her the appearance of a mischievous child playing hide-and-seek in the bedding.

Hosteen and Mary knew Charlie and Betsy Lee very well and they greeted one another warmly. The visitors looked with anxious concern at the sick boy and Hosteen informed them of the Sing scheduled for the next day.

"We'll be there," said Charlie Bigwater and his wife nodded in agreement.

"Let's have some dinner," said Running Bear. Mary got up to help and Harvey handed her the rabbit he had killed earlier but she shook her head, knowing that it was too small to share among five people and that it would deprive Running Bear of his food for the following day. Instead, she prepared frybread, a mixture of flour, baking powder, salt and water, which was patted into cakes and fried in deep fat. Mary also put a pot of fresh coffee on the stove.

There was little conversation until they were all seated around the stove and eating. Before having her own dinner, Mary took the herb tea she had brewed and attempted to spoon it into Joseph Williams's mouth. He seemed to respond slightly, his eyelids fluttering, and he was able to swallow some of the liquid without choking. Mary allowed him to rest for a while and then at intervals fed him a few teaspoons at a time.

"I'll prepare the other medicine when we get home," she said to Hosteen, who nodded his assent.

While they ate, Charlie talked about their visit to the trader. He knew that Betsy Lee was being paid poorly for her labor but it was in immediate cash and that was something they always needed. It was also difficult to sell rugs without having access to tourists and the trader was able to fulfill that function as well. During the past year, Betsy Lee had gotten two direct orders from customers familiar with her work and was able to earn eight times what the trader would have given her. It was the first time that had happened and she hoped that as her fame spread, such orders would make it possible for her to bypass the trader entirely. Since preparing the yarn for a Navajo rug required as much time as it took to actually do the weaving, there was a limit to the number of rugs Betsy Lee could weave in a year.

And with four children at home, all under seven, there never seemed to be enough income.

Throughout the dinner Betsy Lee stole concerned glances at Joseph Williams. The boy looked very ill and illness in a child was something Betsy Lee was very familiar with. She and Charlie had had six children and two had died before their fifth birthdays, one from pneumonia and the other from diarrhea.

Hosteen belched contentedly after he had eaten and rose from his spot on the floor. "It's time to go," he said to Mary. "I want to get down to Tohatchi before it gets too late."

Mary rewrapped Joseph Williams in his hospital blanket while Hosteen went off in a corner with Running Bear and handed him five dollars.

"I will see you at the Sing," said Harvey.

Charlie Bigwater and his wife accompanied Mary and Hosteen to the truck and helped them get settled.

"Do the boy's parents know?" asked Betsy Lee.

"I've sent word," replied Hosteen.

"We'll see you tomorrow then in Tohatchi," said Charlie, shaking hands with Hosteen, who was already in the driver's seat. "And our thoughts will be with you."

The headlights cut a swathe through the cold darkness as the truck pulled away from Running Bear's hogan. Joseph Williams's breathing was easier as they drove to their home twenty miles north. Mary again cradled the boy to her breast and Hosteen turned on the heater. Although it was June, the nights in the desert were still very cold.

"I'll get you home so the boy can have his medicine," said Hosteen. "Then I'll go back to see Sam Begay."

Mary sat silently with Joseph Williams nestled in her arms and watched the full moon rise in the sky. The stars spread out around them in a vast display and Mary felt an inner contentment despite the sick boy being warmed by her body.

CHAPTER 4 _____

IT WAS SHORTLY PAST DAWN WHEN HOSTEEN AND Mary drove up to Sam Begay's hogan with Joseph Williams. There were already a number of pickup trucks and vintage cars parked around the large hexagonal structure and from the hole at the apex of the conical roof, a thin column of smoke rose skyward in the crisp morning air.

An elderly, white-haired man emerged from the hogan as soon as the truck had come to a stop and Hosteen stepped down to greet him. They touched hands briefly without speaking.

Sam Begay wore a flannel shirt and coarse cotton khaki pants. There was nothing about him that would serve to set him apart from any other Navajo elder and despite his seventy years he walked with the gait of a man thirty years younger. He had been a hatali, or Singer, for forty years, having learned his craft from his father, who learned it from his father before him. The Navajos had respected Sam Begay and his ancestors for a century now for their learning. It had taken Sam Begay more than five years of study just to learn one of the two Sings he had mastered. He had attended the Sings conducted by his father and without benefit of a single written word had learned the multitude of long, intricate prayers and songs that made up the curing chantways.

Hosteen took the boy from Mary's arms and helped her down from the truck.

"We can take him inside," said Sam Begay, looking intently at the limp body of the sick child.

They were greeted by at least a dozen people as they entered the large hogan. Harvey Running Bear, Charlie Bigwater and Betsy Lee were already among these early arrivals. Some of the men passed in and out of the hogan carrying armloads of firewood and buckets of water while a group of women sat on the floor kneading dough and patting it into thin slabs of frybread. Mutton and coffee were already cooking on the stove.

Betsy Lee smoothed out a blanket in one corner of the hogan and helped Mary settle the boy on it. His face had a ghostly pallor in the flickering light of the kerosene lamps, giving him the appearance of some sculptor's marble representation of a sleeping Indian youth. Only his sporadic coughing, preceded by the harsh rattle of his breathing, gave evidence that there was still life in his tortured body.

Hosteen in the meantime returned to the truck and brought in an armload of blankets, skins and yardgoods, all part of the payment for the Sing, and these, too, were placed beneath Joseph Williams. Sam Begay joined three of the men, one of whom was Running Bear, sitting near the center of the hogan. Spread out before them was a sand circle at least six feet in diameter and two inches thick. Next to the men were bark receptacles containing charcoal and pulverized minerals to be used in executing the dry painting that was so integral a part of the Navajo curing rites. Other southwestern Indian tribes also used these sandpaintings but the Navajos had developed them to the greatest degree, recognizing somewhere between 500 and 1,000 individual designs.

Sam Begay had consulted the previous evening with Hosteen and together they had selected four designs from the various dry paintings prescribed for the Windways chant. One of these patterns would be created for each of the four days of the ceremonial and then destroyed before sunset.

The artists held the crushed minerals in their right hands and let the powder trickle out from the opening between their thumbs and flexed index fingers. They worked from the center of the picture out toward the periphery in order to avoid disturbing the design. Blue, white, yellow, and black were the colors used and each of these represented a direction. The white was east and the yellow west, while the black and blue symbolized north and south.

The designs in the painting represented the Navajo Holy People and the mystical elements of their belief. Just as Sam Begay's knowledge of the curing ceremonials had been handed down by successive generations, so, too, had the dry painting patterns been handed down by his Singer father and those Singers before him.

There was little opportunity for improvisation in the creation of the designs. Errors made were not erased but were covered over with the neutral color of the background sand.

In the painting taking shape under Sam Begay's direction, one could see the figures of Holy People as well as the four sacred plants—corn, beans, squash and tobacco. When it became necessary to create a straight line two of the men stretched out a cotton string and snapped it between them. The picture was smoothed off at intervals with a narrow strip of wood.

The women in the hogan kept their eyes averted from the painting since it was forbidden for them to witness a sand painting as it was being made.

As the morning wore on, the hogan filled with more and more people and the sound of arriving cars and trucks became a commonplace. Most of the arrivals were members of Mary Begay's clan but there were also numerous friends and acquaintances. Food offerings were carried by all the women but the bulk of the provisions had been supplied by Mary and Hosteen. Hosteen alone had slaughtered thirty sheep during the night and even now his friends were still preparing the carcasses of those that had not yet found their way into the cooking pots. He knew that when the boy's parents arrived they would have already made arrangements for even more food to be delivered.

A large tub had been set up in a corner of the hogan and was filled with greasy chunks of cooked mutton. Each of the guests spooned out the meat with cakes of frybread and then washed it down with coffee. As the cooking of each new batch of mutton was completed, it, too, was unceremoniously dumped into the tub amid the approving nods of the ever-growing crowd.

It was not until midafternoon that Frank and Lilly Williams, the parents of Joseph Williams, arrived from Shiprock. They had driven down in an old Studebaker pickup that had suffered three breakdowns on the way. Behind them was a small convoy of three wood-slatted trucks, each filled with twenty to thirty sheep. There were now close to two hundred people in and around Sam Begay's hogan and the sheep had arrived just in time since the mutton provided by Hosteen was rapidly disappearing.

More than a dozen of the men set themselves the task of

butchering the animals while Frank and Lilly were welcomed into the hogan.

Mary Begay knew that this Sing would be a crushing financial burden to her family. Besides the sheep and the cash payment to the Singer, they had had to purchase buckskins and blankets and herbs for Sam Begay—and it was likely that even more would have to be spent by the clan for additional food to last the four days and three nights. But it would be a Sing to be remembered and no one could accuse her or her family of stinginess.

The dry painting was nearing completion as Frank and Lilly entered the crowded hogan. They were known to all of the people assembled and were greeted warmly. Even as the exchange of greetings occurred, Lilly's glance shifted repeatedly to the figure of her son, almost completely hidden in one corner of the hogan by the large crowd.

After each of the assembled people had welcomed them, they moved quickly toward Joseph Williams. For several minutes, Frank and Lilly stared quietly at the boy, the only sign of their consternation an involuntary movement of Lilly's hand to her mouth as she finally turned to look at her husband. Frank placed his hand sympathetically on her shoulder.

The word had spread to those outside that the prayers were about to begin and a steady stream of people filed into the hogan. Many began taking positions along the walls, with the women, as custom dictated, all sitting on the north side. While Sam Begay put the finishing touches on the Holy People who would intercede for Joseph Williams and restore his world to harmony, his three assistants undressed the boy and carried his limp body to the circle enclosing the painting.

After placing him directly on top of the painting, the three men took their places next to Sam Begay and began to chant the opening prayers of the Windways ceremony.

Sam Begay in the meantime reached over and smeared black coal dust on the boy's body as a dark armor to keep him safe. He then stood and extracted sacred corn pollen from his medicine bundle and sprinkled this around the hogan, threading his way through the tightly assembled group of people.

Returning to his place near the boy, Sam Begay took over the rhythmic chanting and began to tell the story of the Navajo "way."

This narration of the origins of the Navajo people was an integral part of the healing ceremony and reminded those that had gathered for the Sing of where they had come from and where they belonged. Since sickness was a deviation from the ancient ways of the people, the restoration of harmony involved a recapturing of the Navajo "way."

"In the beginning, before there were Earth Surface People, all the holy people lived in other worlds below this one. It took a very long time for them to come up through all the worlds to get here. Here they created all the natural objects, all the mountains and the rocks.

"One of the holy people was Changing Woman. One day she was gathering wood and the Sun touched her. Soon twin sons were born to her and they grew strong and came here to kill the monsters, to make these places safe for the people.

"On one mountain there was an enormous bird who ate people.

"Another monster was a stone man who kicked people off bluffs into the river.

"Near Red Mountain there were insects who paralyzed people by staring at them.

"On other mountains there was a great hollow place where a rock killed people by rolling on them.

"One monster was a spreading canyon and another was a crushing mountain.

"Now the monsters are gone but their places are still here.

"Those like us were made from what was here. The feet and ankles came from the soil of valleys. Man's heart was made from obsidian and his breath white wind. His movement was the air and his tears of rain.

"His face was made of daybreak. Red stones made his nose and his eyes were of sunlight. The new people stayed here where they belong.

"In this place there are still monsters that were not killed. One is Old Age who was spared because some people like her. And Laziness, because sleep is good for people. Also, Thinness, because he hurts no one, and Hunger, because if you starve a little you enjoy good food more. They are still with us.

"Water was brought here to wash the place after all the monsters were killed. In that time, water covered the whole earth except the tops of the mountains. All the trees that were not good enough were washed away and mountains were fastened down with lead and gold. Then new vegetation covered places and everything grew."

Those present had heard this telling of the creation myth of the Navajo people many times. They had heard it in many forms and from many Singers but the basic elements never changed and they never tired of the telling.

A number of the men in the hogan had attended Anglo schools for periods of time and others had served in the United States Army. But they, too, listened intently to Sam Begay's narration and did not question these legends that had been passed down through generations of their forefathers.

From some sacred blankets, Sam Begay now withdrew various herbs—spruce, pinyon, sage, and mint, which he mixed with water and fed to Joseph Williams while Harvey Running Bear supported the boy's head. The child sputtered several times and his eyelids fluttered, but he managed to swallow the medicines.

While Sam Begay ministered to Joseph Williams, another assistant passed community cups of herbs through the crowd. Each person took a few sips, spit into his hands, and then rubbed the mixture on his face and arms.

The chanting continued unabated through each part of the ceremony. Pungent odors hated by ghosts now filled the hogan as Sam Begay set a match to each of the three incense bowls placed around the sandpainting. He then reached once more into his medicine bundle, the same medicine bundle depicted in the sandpainting where a pair of them guarded the eastern entrance to the painting, the only side not protected by a rainbow.

This time he withdrew his bullroarer, a piece of oakwood from a lightning-struck tree, inlaid with turquoise and shells. He began to swing this gift from the Lightning People above his head by means of an attached buckskin thong and a noise like thunder filled the hogan. The evil spirits detested this sound and would have no recourse but to flee from Joseph Williams' body.

The Singer passed the bullroarer to one of his assistants while he himself now took a buffalo-hide rattle covered with eagle feathers, and a hollow reed whistle. As he shook the shells and stones contained within, he touched the rattle to the body of Joseph Williams, each touch punctuated by a loud yelp whose purpose was to frighten the evil spirits and assist the thunder of the bullroarer in driving them out. Intermittently he would blow the whistle to summon the friendly Holy People.

The people in the hogan stared hypnotically at the ceremony transpiring before their eyes. Their bodies swayed almost imperceptibly to the rhythmic chanting and shaking of Sam Begay's rattle.

Now that the evil spirits had been defied, it was time to ensure their departure from their victim's body and to this end Sam Begay touched the feet of the Holy People in the drypainting and touched Joseph Williams's feet, chanting "May his feet be well and restored unto him." Each part of the bodies of the Holy People was touched in turn, and then the Singer's hands touched the corresponding part of the boy's body and prayed for the restoration of well-being for that part.

Not only was Joseph Williams receiving power from the Holy People because of his intimate contact with them, but the sand being placed on each portion of his body was absorbing the evils which had provoked his illness.

When this part of the ceremony was completed, Sam Begay again gave the boy an herb mixture to drink and then tied small pieces of shell and turquoise to his hair so that the supernatural beings would now recognize him as one of their own.

Taking an eagle feather stick to brush away the invisible demons, the Singer now destroyed the sandpainting that he and his assistants had labored for so long to make. He continued to chant prayers as he went about his task. It was necessary to erase it from the center outward, in the order in which it was made, and before sundown. The sand, containing the evils it had absorbed, was now removed from the hogan by one of the assistants to be ceremonially buried.

Many hours had passed since the ceremony had started but no one present was aware of time. Night would soon begin to fall and the desert sky would be filled with stars but to those inside all time had been suspended.

Sam Begay, his lined face showing signs of fatigue from his struggle with the evil spirits and ghosts that plagued the body of Joseph Williams, now stood over the boy and began to recite his final prayer of the evening.

"House made of Dawn!
House made of Evening Light!
House made of Male Rain!
House made of Dark Mists!
House made of Female Rain!
House made of Pollen!
House made of Grasshoppers!
Dark Cloud is at the door.
The outward trail is Dark Cloud.
The zigzag Lightning stands up in it.
Male Deity!
Your offering I make.
I have prepared a smoke for you.
Restore my feet for me!
Restore my legs for me!
Restore my body for me!
Restore my mind for me!
Restore my voice for me!
Your spell remove for me!
You have taken it away for me.
Far off it has gone.
Happily I recover.
Happily my interior becomes cool.
Happily I go forth.
My interior feeling cold, may I walk,
No longer sore, may I walk.
With lively feelings may I walk.
Happily may I walk.
Happily with abundant dark clouds may I walk.
Happily with abundant showers may I walk.
Happily with abundant plants may I walk.
Happily may I walk.
Being as it were to be, long ago may I walk.
May it be happy before me.
May it be beautiful behind me.
May it be beautiful below me.
May it be beautiful above me.
May it be beautiful all around me.
In beauty it is finished, in beauty it is finished."

The people in the hogan seemed to awaken from a trance. For the first time since the ceremony had begun, they became aware of their hunger and the hogan was now a maelstrom of activity with fresh frybread being prepared and chunks of mutton again cooking on the stove. The tub that had earlier been filled with meat was now almost depleted and people surrounded it, anxiously awaiting each new batch of mutton. Campfires had also been started outside the hogan to hasten the cooking.

For Sam Begay and his assistants, there remained, however, a final part to the day's Sing. Joseph Williams would now be given a ceremonial bath in yucca suds and then taken to the sweathouse, a hogan constructed without a smoke hole, in a secluded hollow a short distance from Sam Begay's hogan. Before being given his sweatbath, in which he would be joined by Sam Begay and his assistants, an invitation would be shouted to the Holy People to join in the bath.

This was to be the final purification of the evening. The next day, and for two days after that, the ritual would be repeated.

On this first night, and on the following one, most of the people would go back to their homes. Some would not return but there would be others to take their place. On the final evening of the Sing, the chanting and praying would continue throughout the night. Most of those present would take part in the sweatbath and many would take emetics to aid in their purification.

On the fourth and last day the family of Joseph Williams would walk across the last sandpainting, following in the footsteps of the Holy People.They, too, would come into the same close communion with the Holy People as Joseph Williams. And the boy himself would walk among the ranks of the Holy People, once again in complete harmony with his universe, free of the evils that now tortured him.

CHAPTER 5 _____

JOHN HARTMAN SAT IN HIS OFFICE AND READ THE social service note on his latest admission.

"Sammy Redwing is fourteen and for the past five years has lived with an uncle in Manuelito. The uncle is unemployed and an alcoholic. Sammy's own father was killed in an accident about eight years ago and his mother died of tuberculosis five years ago. Since moving in with his uncle Sammy has not attended school. He occasionally does "farmwork" when it is available. For the past three or four years he has been drinking heavily, both wine and liquor. His uncle apparently offers no objection and is 'usually too drunk to care anyway' or invites the boy to drink with him."

The remainder of the note dealt with the possibilities of placement after the patient had recovered and been discharged, and this portion John scanned quickly before closing the folder and dropping it on his desk. He knew that the prospects for placement were bleak, if not impossible for an adolescent Navajo alcoholic.

Sammy Redwing had been admitted with acute alcohol intoxication and for the first twenty-four hours it had been touch and go. The Peds service had already lost three boys sixteen or under with the same problem during the first five months of the year and John Hartman had feared that Sammy would be the fourth. With intensive treatment, however, his condition had stabilized and he now appeared to be out of the woods, for this admission at least. Sammy Redwing was a prime candidate for cirrhosis of the liver before the age of twenty.

John Hartman had done a year of internship at Massachusetts General and had had no dearth of experience with alcoholics on the medical service. He had treated scores of patients from the Irish and black ghettoes of Boston, men and women who had been admitted with delirium tremens or acute intoxication or cirrhosis. He had seen patients die in the throes of psychosis induced by alcohol and he had seen others exsanguinate from massive bleeding due to rupture of the dilated veins of the esophagus. But he had never seen a patient with these problems under the age of thirty—until he came to Gallup.

Upon his arrival he had listened with incredulity to the stories about eighteen year olds with cirrhosis and boys in their early teens dying of an alcohol binge. But after more than three years of working with Navajo patients he now accepted all of it as a fact of life. There were many abhorrent facts he had been compelled to accept since joining the Indian Health Service. His emotions had run the gamut from rage to frustration to bitterness. Now he simply tried to do the best he could within a system that had few answers to the overwhelming problems with which he was confronted almost on a daily basis.

"Come in," he called in response to a knock on his office door. A bald-headed man opened the door slowly and peeked in.

"Hi, Vince, come on in."

Vincent Ambrosino had been supervisor of the laboratory almost since the hospital had first opened its doors. He was a timid-looking man and the troubled expression on his lean, angular face only exaggerated the frailty of his appearance.

"John, we have trouble," he said softly.

"Don't we always?" asked John, smiling in spite of himself. He knew how sensitive Vincent was and always tried to adopt a serious demeanor when speaking to him.

Vincent looked even more crestfallen now and John thought that he would burst into tears at any moment.

"Oh, come on, Vincent," he said finally with some exasperation. "It can't be all that bad."

Vincent nodded. "Oh, yes it can. You have a patient named Joseph Williams?"

"Had would be a better word. The boy's grandmother pulled him out of the hospital the same day he was admitted—that was two days ago."

"Oh, God!" exclaimed Vincent. He reached out to the door frame for support.

John looked at him curiously. Even if he was accustomed to Vincent's morose behavior, he had never seen him act like this. "Hey, come on, sit down," he called, "and tell me about it." He pushed the chair next to his desk toward Vincent, who needed no further invitation and slumped heavily into it.

"John, look, we have the culture reports on the kid's blood and sputum." His hand trembled as he fished the reports out of his pocket and offered them to John. He then watched the doctor's face intently as the reports were read. When John Hartman again looked up Vincent was inwardly pleased to see that his reports had made the impact he anticipated. The color had completely drained out of the young pediatrician's face.

"Vincent, are you sure of this?"

"John, we did fluorescent antibody stains and every culture was positive. I've sent additional cultures to the CDC in Fort Collins but there's no doubt. It's Yersinia pestis. The boy has plague. And now—" He gestured with his arm toward the window. "He's out there somewhere."

"Vince, this kid had an obvious pneumonitis, so we're dealing with plague pneumonia!" He shook both of his fists in anger. "Damn that Mary Begay!"

"Who's that?"

"The kid's grandmother. We tried to convince her to leave the boy here with us but she wouldn't listen."

John recalled his conversations with Bill Moore and Sam Spencer after the woman had carried her grandson out of the hospital and a flush of embarrassment came to his cheeks.

"Look, Vincent, I'll keep these reports and I'm going down to see Mr. Oliver. Don't say anything to anyone about this for the time being. We'll have to find Joseph Williams if he's still alive and we're also going to have to arrange antibiotic prophylaxis for everyone in the hospital who was in contact with the boy."

"What about all the people the boy's been in contact with outside the hospital?"

"Don't remind me," he called, hurrying past Vincent. He was out the door before Vincent could stand up but then suddenly poked his head back in. "By the way, Vincent—good work!"

Vincent sat back in the chair with a look of contentment on his face. He hoped John would put in a good word for him to Mr. Oliver, too. Being a true scientist certainly has its drawbacks, he mused, suddenly becoming fretful again. There's so seldom any praise given for a job well done.

John Hartman paced nervously while awaiting the elevator and after no more than ten seconds took the stairs instead. He walked quickly down the corridor to the Administrator's office and did not wait to be announced by Russell Oliver's astonished secretary. The woman started to protest but John was already past her and entering Oliver's office. The Adminstrator held a golf club and was in his putting stance as John entered. He looked up in surprise, momentarily disconcerted, then quickly recovered his composure when he saw who it was.

"I didn't hear the buzzer ring. Isn't my secretary at her desk?"

John ignored the question. "Sir, we have a serious problem."

"You're goddamn right we do. If I miss any more short putts like the two I blew yesterday, I'll probably have a nervous breakdown."

"Do you remember that boy brought to the hospital by the Secretary of State earlier in the week?"

"Yes. Wasn't that the damndest thing you ever heard of? The Secretary of State of the United States of America walking into an Indian Hospital in Gallup, New Mexico, with a sick Indian kid. I had a hell of a time convincing my friends that he was really here. Did you see the pictures of him in today's paper? He was shaking hands with—"

"Mr. Oliver," interrupted John, "the boy has plague."

The Administrator blinked and his lips silently repeated the words. He leaned the golf club against his desk and stared at John. "You mean like bubonic plague?"

"Even worse," said John. "He's got a plague pneumonia—pneumonic plague. It's very contagious and it's deadly."

"But, are you sure of this?"

"We have a positive bacteriologic diagnosis from Vincent Ambrosino."

"Oh, hell, what does Vincent know about plague?"

"Sir, Vincent says it is plague."

"Well, how's the boy doing?"

"I don't know."

"What do you mean you don't know?"

"His grandmother pulled him out of the hospital the same day he came in."

"What the hell for?"

"She wanted him to have a Sing."

"Oh, Christ! The goddamn ignorant bastards! They never learn. Why didn't you tell me this before? That was days ago."

"We didn't know then what the boy had. It's not the first time that patients have been taken out of the hospital to see the Singer."

"Well, goddamn it, now what?" Russell Oliver's face was flushed with anger as he picked up his golf club and walked to his chair.

"Well, first of all we'd better try to locate the boy. It's more than likely that he's already expired but we have to know who his contacts are. And we have to begin antibiotic prophylaxis for everyone in the hospital who had contact with the boy."

"Have you heard of anyone coming down with any symptoms?"

"No, but we'd better check to see if any of the staff is out sick."

"Okay, get on it right away and get anyone you need to help you."

"There's one other thing. I don't think we should let word of this leak out—it might lead to panic."

"How the hell are you going to check on all the people who were in contact with the kid without telling them anything?"

"We could just say that the boy had a contagious type of pneumonia. People don't respond very rationally when they hear the word 'plague.'"

"What if we do get other cases?"

"Then we'll have to let it be known. But for the time being I think it would be better to handle it this way. Can you imagine the newspapers getting hold of this? The word 'plague' would be in six inch letters in every headline and we'd have mass hysteria."

"What about that blabbermouth Vincent?"

"I've already warned him not to say anything—I'll tell him again."

"Tell him I'll string him up by his balls if he opens his mouth."

John suppressed a smile, nodded, and left the office as Oliver remained sitting moodily at this desk. He headed immediately to the Personnel Office.

Beth Rodriguez, the personnel director, was on the phone as

John entered. She smiled at him and covered the mouthpiece of the receiver with her hand. "What a nice surprise—I'll be off in a minute."

John sat down in a chair opposite Beth and watched her as she spoke. Beth was half-Mexican, half-Navajo. She had a dark, exotic beauty that reminded him of Valentina. Her eyes were large with the longest lashes he had ever seen and her lips full and sensuous. She wore her thick black hair in a long ponytail. John guessed that she was about twenty-seven but actually he knew nothing about her, except for some gossip he had overhead one day in the cafeteria when it was mentioned that she was divorced. He himself had only spoken to her several times over coffee in the four or five months she had worked at the hospital and those conversations invariably revolved around hospital trivia. He hadn't dated since Valentina's death and he had thought of asking Beth out but was deterred by his own shyness and, even more, by his persistent feeling of complicity in Valentina's death.

Fixing his gaze on her lips, he wondered what it would be like to kiss her. The thought provoked definite sexual yearnings and he squirmed uncomfortably in his chair.

She hung up and laughed. "That silly sister of mine is too much. She's getting married this Sunday and can't decide if she's supposed to be happy or miserable. Well, I guess it's normal to be nervous as the day approaches. But I know you're not here to listen to me talk about my sister's wedding. You're not looking for a different job, are you?" she asked jokingly.

"Sometimes I think it wouldn't be a bad idea," he replied, smiling.

"Uh, oh, sounds like a bad day. Anything I can help you with?"

"Yes, I think so, Beth. It's very important that I know if anyone has reported in sick in the past two days and then not returned to work."

She looked at him in surprise. "Are we starting a campaign against malingerers?"

"No," he laughed. "But it's very important. How soon do you think you could get that information for me?"

"Well, I'll have to call each department head and the supervisor on every floor. Do you want it limited to any particular departments or should I check with all of them?"

John thought for a moment. "You'd better check them all."

"Okay." She looked at her watch. "Can you give me a half hour or so?"

"Sure. I'll take care of some other business and then I'll be back."

He waved and called "thanks" as he left the office to head over to Social Services. Walking down the hall, John carried with him the image of Beth's flashing white teeth and the delightful sound of her laugh. His thoughts dwelled on the singular beauty of her face and the Indian voluptuousness of her body. There was no denying that she stimulated him as no woman had since Valentina's death. Guilt or no guilt, he knew he wanted to ask her out. To be continued, he said to himself, as he entered Tom Whitman's office and brought his attention back to the business at hand.

Tom Whitman was a gentle bearded giant of a man. Originally from Nebraska, he had long been interested in Native Americans and prior to coming to Gallup had done his social work among the Oglala Sioux and Cherokees. He eased his six-feet six-inch frame out from behind his desk and shook hands warmly with John.

"How goes the healing art, John?"

"Rather badly at the moment, Tom."

Tom's bushy blond moustache and beard were split by a grin. "Don't tell me that your little charges are getting to you all of a sudden."

"Not all of them. Just one. We have a serious problem that I hope you can help us with. Earlier this week a young Navajo boy, about ten or eleven, was brought into the hospital unconscious. Before we could complete our workup, his grandmother carried him out of the hospital to see the Singer. We've gotten back the laboratory work and we have reason to believe the boy has a serious, highly contagious disease. The problem now is to find him and the people who've been in contact with him."

"I see," said Tom, sitting down at his desk and picking up a pad and pencil. "Do you have the boy's name?"

"His name is Joseph Williams. The grandmother's name is Mary Begay. But we have no addresses."

Tom whistled softly. "Williams and Begay. That's like trying to find Jones and Smith. Anything else that might provide a lead?"

John thought for a moment. "There is one thing. The boy was brought in by Sam Spencer, the Secretary of State—"

"Ah ," interrupted Tom, "then the story is true. I heard all about it, of course, but many of the people here thought that it was just a rumor."

"No, it's true, all right. Apparently the boy's horse was hit by a car just outside of town. Spencer happened to be driving by and brought the boy here."

"Did anyone else see the accident?"

"Spencer mentioned that some of the Indian locals were around waiting for the bars to open."

"Now we're getting somewhere. So the boy had a horse and was seen by some Indians. There's a chance that one of them may have recognized him."

"It's more than likely," agreed John. "How else could Mary Begay have found out that the boy was brought here? But how will we be able to find the person who knew him?"

"Leave that to me, old buddy. I can't promise anything but I'll do my best. Incidentally, what do you think the kid has?"

John hesitated. He knew he could take Tom into his confidence but it had been, after all, his own decision not to let the word get out.

"I'm sorry, Tom, but I'm not at liberty to say. Orders from Oliver."

"Sounds very serious."

"It is."

"Okay, I'll get on it right away and be back in touch with you. I hope to have some news for you by the afternoon."

John left Tom Whitman's office feeling that if anyone could locate the boy, it was Tom. He was the only Anglo John had ever met whom the Indians appeared to trust completely. It wasn't simply that he was interested in them and spoke Navajo almost flawlessly, although that was certainly true. For years, he had immersed himself in the life of the Indians, not only as a scholar but also as a participant. He understood them and, even more important, he did not pass judgement. Indian culture was as "right" as Anglo culture and he supported them fully, whether they resisted Anglo advances or decided to accept those they wished to assimilate. John was convinced that the Indians recognized this unique tolerance by an Anglo and responded to it by accepting Tom as one of their own.

His buoyed spirits were dealt a blow, however, when he returned to Beth's office and was presented with a list of three names.

"These are the only three who reported in sick. Ted Johnson, one of the orderlies, is an asthmatic and that's apparently what his problem is now. But I don't know about Lee Medina and Emma Hastings. Someone called for them and in each case reported that it was the flu."

John felt a sudden tingling at the base of his scalp. Both Lee and Emma and been in close contact with the boy. It could just be coincidental, but it was not a time for assumptions.

"Beth, would you give me their addresses and phone numbers, please." Beth was about to engage in some light banter about his excessive concern, but seeing the expression on his face she changed her mind and went to her files. She wrote the addresses and phone numbers down for him. Emma lived in Gallup and Lee just outside of town.

"Good," nodded John. "Both of them pretty close."

"Would I be accused of a lack of tact if I asked what was going on?"

"I wish I could tell you but I can't. Perhaps in a few days if all goes well."

Puzzled, Beth smiled. "It all sounds so mysterious."

John looked at his watch. "I'd better run." He hesitated for a moment and then blurted out what was in his mind. "Beth, can I interest you in dinner some evening?"

"Why, Dr. Hartman, I thought you'd never ask. Of course. When shall we go?"

"How about tomorrow evening? I know that's short notice."

"Tomorrow would be fine. Would you like to pick me up at home about seven?"

He nodded and she wrote her address and phone number for him. "It's only about ten minutes from the hospital."

"We'd better start thinking which of Gallup's coffee shops mutilates food the least," laughed John, relieved now that Beth had accepted his invitation.

"I have a better idea—how about my preparing dinner? Do you like Mexican food?"

"Love it, but I don't want you to go to that—"

"It's no bother," she said. "I like to cook and I can outdo any Gallup coffee shop."

John laughed. "I'll see you tomorrow then."

"Good luck on your house calls," she said as he went out the door.

John returned to the ward to pick up his medical bag. He arranged for one of the other physicians to cover him while he was out of the hospital, then debated whether to call Oliver. I'll reach him later if I have to, he decided, while descending in the elevator, and headed directly out into the parking lot to his car.

Emma Hastings lived in a simple white adobe house on Second Street. John knew she was a widow and that she lived with an older sister, who had moved to Gallup at the time of Emma's husband's death. They were among the handful of blacks living in the town. John knocked on the door and waited. There was no sound within the house and he knocked again. This time the door opened a crack and a grey-haired black woman peeked out.

"Is Emma Hastings at home?" asked John.

"She's very sick," the woman replied.

"Yes, I know. That's why I've come to see her. I'm Dr. Hartman. I work with Emma at the hospital."

The woman was obviously relieved and opened the door.

"I don't know what to do for her. She's so sick," she clucked as she led John along a short corridor that separated the kitchen from a room whose door was closed. The house was gloomy and dark with very little light filtering through the drawn window shades. John followed her through the living room, sparsely furnished with timeworn overstuffed chairs, and on into a bedroom at the rear of the house.

The light in the room was so dim that John could barely make out the form in the bed. He could hear the woman's rapid, hard breathing and the sounds of the bedsprings creaking every time she moved.

"Can you put on a light for me?" he asked.

There was no overhead light and the woman fumbled with the switch of a small lamp set on a night table to one side of the bed.

John looked down at the sweating, agitated face of Emma Hastings, a nurse with whom he had worked since he first arrived at the hospital. Her eyes were open but she was obviously unaware of his presence. Her lips moved, mumbling incoherent words, and she squirmed uncomfortably in the bed, flailing her arms each time she turned.

John felt her forehead, then picked up her limp wrist to take her pulse. She was obviously burning with fever and her pulse rate was a thready 160 per minute.

Emma groaned suddenly and her body began to shake in a dry paroxysm of coughing.

"How long has she been like this?" asked John.

"It started night before last, replied the sister. "She said her chest hurt her when she breathed or moved. She tried to go to work yesterday morning but her knees hurt a lot and she felt bad all over. Then the fever came and she started breathing funny. I didn't know what to do. I had the flu last year but it weren't this bad. Will she be all right, doctor?"

"Let me have a look at her," he replied, pulling back the covers. He applied the blood pressure cuff to her arm and pumped it up. Her pressure was 100 over 80, which seemed low for her age but John did not know the reading she usually ran. He used a tongue depressor to open her mouth and found the mucous membranes to be dry but there was no sign of any throat inflammation. He felt carefully for any lymph node swelling but could detect none. Except for the rapid rate, examination of her heart was normal. Her lungs, however, were filled with coarse rhonchi and she had a prolonged expiratory wheeze. Her respirations were labored at about thirty a minute and it was evident that she was having serious difficulty breathing.

John placed his stethoscope back in his bag and covered Emma with the blanket. He turned to look at her sister, who stood behind him wringing her hands and silently moving her lips. John thought she might be praying.

"Your sister is very sick," he said softly. "We'll have to take her to the hospital. Can I use your phone?"

The woman nodded and pointed toward the living room. John glanced once more at Emma before leaving the room. He knew that he was looking at a dying woman and that it would no longer be possible to maintain silence once the diagnosis was proven.

He requested an ambulance and then spoke to the physician on duty in the emergency room. Without going into too many details, John informed him that he was sending in a critically ill patient, one of the hospital's nursing staff, and that he wanted her placed in strict isolation with respiratory quarantine. "Get in touch with Bill Moore," he continued, "and have him see her. Tell him I hope to be there within the hour. Also, call Mr. Oliver and inform him about this patient's admission. Give him the same message as the one to Bill, that I'll see him soon."

John placed the receiver softly back on its hook, deliberately trying not to violate the silence of the house. He walked back into the bedroom and found the old woman standing motionless where he had left her.

"Is she going to die, doctor?" she asked, her voice scarcely audible.

John placed his hand gently on her shoulder. "She is very sick. An ambulance should be here in just a few minutes. When we get her to the hospital, we'll do all we can for her. Your sister is a wonderful woman and a fine nurse. We all love her and she'll be well taken care of."

The woman nodded, listening more to what was not being said. Tears rolled down her cheeks and John felt his own throat tighten.

"There is one thing I must ask of you," he said. "Please don't leave the house for the next four days. One of us will be dropping off an antibiotic for you to take. And I promise to get in touch with you by this evening to let you know how your sister is."

"Can't I go to the hospital to be with my sister? she asked.

"Your sister won't be allowed any visitors. Her illness is very contagious. That's why I don't want you to leave the house, just in case you're carrying the infection. It would only spread it. I want you to check your temperature twice a day and call me if it's elevated. When you get your antibiotic today, I want you to take it every six hours for the next six days. We'll be calling you every day to see how you're doing and to tell you about Emma. Let us know if there's anything you need and we'll bring it to you."

The woman turned from him and stared at her sister. A look of helpless resignation had settled on her face.

"Oh, one more thing," said John. "Please don't allow any visitors into the house for the next four days except for me or one of the other doctors. I know that it will be difficult for you but it's so very important. As soon as we know that there's no longer any danger of the infection spreading, we'll tell you.

"I've got to go now to see another patient. Will you be all right?"

"Yes," she whispered. "Thank you."

John left her at her sister's bedside and walked back through the quiet gloom of the house to the front door. He knew he should probably have alerted Bill Moore and Russell Oliver personally on the phone but he did not want to waste any time. There was still Lee Medina to be seen and he dreaded what he would find there. Once he had examined the Medina girl he could head back to the hospital and meet with Bill and Oliver.

He drove rapidly now west on Highway 66, watching the motels and gas stations become further and further apart as he left the environs of Gallup. The road on which Lee's house was located was only about three miles outside of the town and he watched carefully to avoid missing his turnoff. It must have been somewhere along here, he thought, that Spencer had picked up Joseph Williams. Now it appeared that the deed of a good samaritan had set off a chain of events that threatened the lives of many of the hospital staff. John suddenly felt his own vulnerability. Never before in his medical career had he thought about the possibility of personal danger despite repeated contact with patients suffering from serious infectious diseases. Plague, however, was different. The word itself, even when used in a general sense, connoted a terrible affliction. Throughout the course of history the pneumonic form of plague had decimated entire populations each time it made its appearance. This was the same infection that had killed 25 million people in Europe alone during the fourteenth century. John gave an involuntary shudder as he remembered the grimly appropriate appelation earned by the disease—"the Black Death."

"Well, nothing to do but start some Tetracycline when I get back to the hospital, then wait and see," he said aloud, using the sound of his own voice to allay the apprehension he felt. At least he was forewarned and if symptoms were to develop, immediate threatment with the appropriate antibiotic could be instituted. But he knew that even this did not guarantee a cure of one of the most lethal infections known.

He spotted the Pecos Road sign on the left of the highway and swung off onto a narrow two-lane road whose macadam quickly gave way to an unpaved, washboarded surface. Clouds of dust swirled around his car as he bounced along for an agonizing half-mile, until at last he saw an adobe house with the name Medina on the mailbox.

The structure was surrounded by a yard of almost pure sand. Except for brown scrub and occasional wild cactus, there were no trees or other green shrubs. It was a far cry from the forested areas of New England and palm tree-laced San Diego, he thought. He noticed as he walked toward the house, carrying his medical bag, that a few clay flower pots were set on a windowsill, each with a diminutive plant struggling to survive in the summer heat. One had even managed to produce some frail pink blooms that resembled begonia, the solitary expression of color in an otherwise drab and lifeless landscape.

Before he could knock, the door opened suddenly and he was confronted by a Mexican woman dressed in black. He guessed that it was Lee's mother and that the woman was really younger than her lined brown face would indicate. Her eyes were inflamed and he assumed she had conjunctivitis, a common malady in the area because of the windblown sand and the presence of small black gnats that swarmed everywhere at certain times of the year carrying the infection from one victim to the next.

She looked at him questioningly.

"I'm Dr. Hartman. I work with Lee at the hospital and I understand she's sick. May I see her?" He spoke slowly, uncertain if she would understand.

"Ai, doctor," wailed the woman, "mi hija esta tan enferma," and she began to cry, using one corner of the shawl around her shoulders to wipe the tears away. John's grasp of Spanish was sufficient to understand her expression of concern and he knew now that what he had mistaken for conjunctivitis was probably caused by the grieving the woman had done for her sick daughter.

"Venga, pase usted," she said, leading him into the house. A young woman of about twenty appeared from the kitchen holding a dishtowel. "Es mi otra hija, Catalina," said Lee's mother and she rapidly explained in Spanish to this other daughter who John was.

"I'm glad you've come," she said. "I was going to call the hospital today to see if one of the doctors could see my sister. She's been sick for the past two days. I thought she had the flu but now I don't know. She coughs a lot and she's been spitting up blood. I hope it's not TB."

Catalina led him to a small bedroom that she apparently shared with her sister. From one of the two beds, Lee stared wide-eyed at him, an anxious expression on her flushed face. "Oh, Doctor Hartman," she exclaimed weakly. "I'm so—" Her words were interrupted by a fit of coughing, and a stream of watery sputum, flecked with blood, ran down her chin.

He took her hand in his and felt the heat emanating from her body. "I have a high fever," she said in a hoarse whisper and tears welled in her eyes. "I'm afraid I'm going to die."

John gently stroked her forehead. "We won't let that happen, Lee. Let me check you over and see what's going on."

The temperature patch he placed on her forehead indicated 104.6. Her pulse was racing at 140 a minute but appeared to be strong.

"When did she become sick?" he asked Catalina.

"She didn't feel well yesterday morning. She had fever and said she ached all over." Lee nodded, corroborating her sister's words. "Then she got a bad headache and after that it began to hurt when she breathed. She was too sick to go to work. Then last night she began to cough a lot and we noticed some blood in her phlegm."

Mrs. Medina stood behind them, struggling to follow her older daughter's English. After each sentence, she turned toward John to see what effect, if any, the words had on him.

Catalina helped John remove her sister's nightgown and he conducted his usual methodical examination. All the signs of the girl's infection were localized to her lungs, and although John was convinced that Lee had the same disease as Emma Hastings, he felt that at least here there was still a chance to combat the infection in time. Lee's younger and stronger body seemed to be putting up a better struggle against the virulent enemy trying to destroy it.

John spoke calmly to her, trying to eliminate any excessive concern from his voice. "Lee, you have an infection in your lungs and we're going to treat you in the hospital. I'm sure that—" He paused as once again the girl appeared to be on the verge of tears. Taking both her hands in his, he smiled reassuringly at her. "Lee, you're going to be all right. I'm going to call an ambulance from the hospital because I think you're too weak to make the trip in my car. We'll have you in the hospital in less than an hour and then we'll start treating your infection."

"You don't think I'm going to die?" she asked, her words almost inaudible.

"Lee, you don't believe that I'm going to allow us to lose the best lab technician in the hospital, do you?" He patted her arm. "We'll pull you through this. Trust me."

She gave an almost imperceptible nod and for a moment a smile flickered on her lips. Some of the tension evident in her face appeared to ebb and she closed her eyes, falling asleep almost immediately.

John turned to Mrs. Medina. "May I use your phone?"

"Si, doctor," replied the woman, leading him to the wall phone in the kitchen. Catalina had apparently been chopping up onions and chili peppers to make a sauce and the eyesmarting vapors were heavy in the air. John dialed the hospital number and rubbed his eyes while waiting for the operator to answer. It's amazing any bacteria could survive in this environment, he thought.

Again he spoke to Doug Harris, the emergency room physician, requesting an ambulance and relaying the same instructions he had given earlier for Emma Hastings.

"Hey, John, what the hell kind of an epidemic are you bringing into this hospital?" asked Harris. "That nurse, Hastings, was almost moribund when she got here. Both Bill Moore and Oliver came down to see her. She's in isolation on the ward now but I don't think she's going to make it. Bill wants to talk to you and Oliver is having fits."

"Doug, listen. Tell them I'm leaving Lee Medina's house right now and heading back to the hospital. I'll be there in about fifteen or twenty minutes and I'll talk to them as soon as I get there."

He replaced the receiver and rejoined Catalina and her mother in the bedroom.

"An ambulance should be here in a few minutes. Because we don't want other people to get the infection, Lee will be in a room by herself and no visitors will be allowed. I'll call you by this evening though to let you know how she's doing. Since you've both been exposed to the infection, I don't want either of you to leave the house for the next four days and you shouldn't admit any visitors except for the doctors who come here. Either I or one of the other doctors will be coming back later to bring you an antibiotic to take. You'll take it every six hours for six days. Also check your temperature a couple of times a day and call me if it goes up. We'll be calling you every day to see how you're doing."

"I understand," said Catalina. "What kind of infection do you think it is?"

"We'll have to do some tests to make sure and then I'll be able to tell you."

"Do you think my mother and I will get it, too?"

"I'm hoping that the antibiotic will prevent that. That's why we'll be checking with you each day. At the first sign of any problem, we can treat you. Catalina, please reassure your mother and tell her everything will be all right. If you need anything here, let me know and I'll arrange to have it brought to you."

He walked back to the bed and stroked Lee's forehead, moving the strands of hair matted to her skin by perspiration.

"Do you really think she'll be all right?" asked Catalina softly, a tremor in her voice.

"I can't promise anything but I do think she has a fighting chance. I'll head back to the hospital now to get everything ready for Lee's arrival."

"Thank you," said Catalina, shaking his hand. Mrs. Medina also took his hand in hers and again began to cry. "Gracias, doctor, gracias por todo."

On the drive back to the hospital John evaluated what he knew so far about the potentially lethal infection that threatened everyone who had been in contact with young Joseph Williams. Although the boy himself probably had the bubonic variety of the disease with secondary development of a plague pneumonia, everyone else was threatened with primary plague pneumonia due to the respiratory transmission of the bacteria.

There had been numerous reports of plague in the United States in the twentieth century, predominantly in the southwest, but these were usually sporadic cases associated with wild rodents. Fleas were the vector carrying the infection to man and the result was the bubonic form of the disease, causing no serious risk to other human beings--unless plague pneumonia developed, as had occurred with Joseph Williams. This resulted in direct transmission to others with the resultant fulminant primary pneumonia he had seen in Emma Hastings and Lee Medina. John knew that untreated patients with plague pneumonia rarely survived more than three days. It would take a miracle to save Emma Hastings and he was sure that Joseph Williams was already dead. Lee Medina's chances for survival were fifty-fifty, at best. How many other people were at risk of developing the disease? Certainly every doctor and nurse who had had intimate contact with Joseph Williams—that meant himself, Bill Moore, the nurses on the Pediatric floor and those in the clinic where the boy was first seen. Then there were the lab technicians, but so far as he knew, Lee was the only one who had been with the boy. The secretarial personnel and X-Ray technicians were at lesser risk. At least six people had originally been exposed while ministering to the boy. Two of those people had already contracted the disease. He also had to consider the additional staff that were now attending to Emma Hastings and that soon would be in contact with Lee Medina. The original half dozen at greatest risk had surely doubled, and with each new case there was the possibility of involving a growing number of hospital personnel.

Nevertheless, John forced himself to take a more sanguine outlook. If the remaining four people who had been in contact with Joseph Williams could somehow manage to escape the infection and if another two or three days went by with no new cases, then there would be a very real chance of coping with the outbreak. The institution of antibiotic prophylaxis and the use of respiratory quarantine should also help contain the spread of the disease.

The family of Joseph Williams was another matter. It was impossible to know how many people, besides Mary Begay, had been in contact with the boy. The intrusion of that thought into John's calculations led him to wonder if he was deluding himself in the hope that the spread of the disease could be contained. Only when he was able to locate Mary Begay would he be able to know the real magnitude of the problem, and the only chance of success there rested with Tom Whitman, who he hoped would have some information for him by the time he returned to the hospital.

His thoughts suddenly turned to Beth Rodriguez and for the first time since leaving the hospital his face relaxed into a smile. He barely knew Beth and yet he felt that he had met a woman who held out the promise of what had been absent from his life for the past three years—an intimacy and a sharing. His hopes might be premature but the very fact that he could even contemplate Beth in this way was a turning point in his own life. After the breakup of his marriage, and especially after the death of Valentina, guilt had been the emotion that consumed him. It had led him to avoid, until now, any relationship that held even a hint of potential intimacy.

There were times, in the first months after his arrival at the Indian Health Center, when self-pity and loneliness led him to question his decision to join the Indian Health Service. Initially, he knew, he had used it as an escape from San Diego and from the death of Valentina. And he also knew that professionally he could not have asked for more than what awaited him in Boston—there had been offers of partnership after completion of his residency, the availability of the finest hospitals in the country, and the certainty of a successful pediatric practice. The problem, he believed, was in the definition of success. If it were to be measured financially or by the recognition received from colleagues, then undoubtedly Boston would have offered him all that. As the months passed in Gallup, however, John became aware that for the first time in his medical career he felt truly needed. The children of Boston needed physicians, too, but if there were no John Hartman there would be numerous alternatives, scores of pediatricians and clinics. The Navajos did not have the luxury of alternatives. John never deluded himself into believing for a moment that he was indispensable but he did know that if he were to leave Gallup, his skills at the Indian Medical Center would be sorely missed. He was also aware that the void created in the health care of Navajo children by his departure from Dinetah would be accompanied by a similar emptiness in his own life.

And so, John Hartman had developed his own definition of success. It meant being needed by a people who were out of the mainstream of American life and who desperately depended on his knowledge and abilities—and that provided the accomplishment and satisfaction that he sought in his profession.

He knew that had Valentina lived she would have willingly shared his life in Gallup. Her professional talents, too, would have been indispensable at the hospital. But that was not to be. And even though he still loved her with an intensity that was painful to think about, he was beginning to realize that the guilt he had felt all these years after her death served no purpose. It only acted as a crippling impediment to getting on with the rest of his life.

Suddenly he became aware that he was in the hospital parking lot, easing his old Ford into a space near the entrance. He sat quietly for several moments after removing the key from the ignition. The immediate future, he knew, promised to be difficult. This plague epidemic was going to require all of his energies and abilities in the fight to contain it. But when he thought of the future in a general sense, for the first time in longer than he could remember he felt anything was possible. And it was Beth Rodriguez, he knew, who was responsible for that feeling.

Walking up the ramp toward the main entrance, his gaze unconsciously shifted toward the windows of the office where he knew Beth was working at that very minute. And it was at that very minute that he heard his name shouted by a familiar voice.

Russell Oliver was standing in the entranceway, his appearance apoplectic. "Follow me," he said angrily as John approached. John followed him into his office and Oliver slammed the door.

"It's about time you got here. Do you have any idea what's going on?"

John had never seen the Administrator like this. His lips were trembling with rage and little bubbles of spittle were now present in the corners of his mouth.

"Yes," he replied, trying to keep his voice calm. "We have two cases of probable pneumonic plague."

"Two, hell!" exclaimed Oliver, his face beet-red. "Goddamn it, John, we have four. Four cases of plague!"

"Four!" John was stunned.

"Yes, four. Elsie Sims and Andrea Eagle, two nurses from the Pediatrics ward, were also brought in while you were gone."

"Oh, Christ," gasped John weakly.

"Bill Moore has been calling down here every five minutes to find out if you've come back. I didn't know what to tell him but he suspects you know what's going on. What the hell are we going to do now? We can't keep the goddamn thing a secret from the chief of medicine. This fucking plague is liable to wipe out the whole damn hospital." He paused suddenly and looked intently at John. "And by the way, how are you feeling?"

"So far, so good," replied John, smiling in spite of himself at the sudden show of concern after Oliver's outburst. "I'll go talk to Bill now. I agree with you. It's past the point where we can keep our suspicions secret but we still have to try to avert a panic. And hopefully keep it out of the newspapers. We're going to have to get everyone who's had contact with the Indian boy or with new cases on prophylactic antibiotics. After I talk to Bill, we'll set up a meeting with medical staff, all heads of departments and all nursing supervisors to talk about prophylaxis and quarantine measures.

"The next big problem is finding who on the reservation was in contact with Joseph Williams. I've got Tom Whitman working on that. Then we can set up antibiotic prophylaxis through the clinic and a surveillance system on the reservation.

"Then there are the contacts of our present cases. I've explained to the families of Lee Medina and Emma Hastings that they're not to leave their homes or admit visitors. We'll get them on antibiotics today and we'll check with them daily to make sure they're okay. We're going to have to do the same thing with the families of the two new admissions."

"Andrea was brought in by her husband and Elsie by her brother. Both the men are still here with them as far as I know. Bill tells me that all four patients are sick as hell."

"Okay, I'll take care of everything when I talk to Bill. The only chance we've got with this disease besides trying to prevent it is spotting the cases early, isolating them while they're being treated, and keeping the contacts isolated, too."

John took the stairs two at a time up to the medical floor and found a flurry of activity occasioned by the four new admissions. Patients were also being removed from other two-bed rooms in case these, too, would have to be requisitioned, and were being transferred to the larger wards. Two of the semi-private rooms had been occupied by the four infected patients and John was pleased to see that strict respiratory precautions were in effect. Anyone entering the rooms had to be gowned, gloved and masked.

Bill Moore and another internist, Jeff Grant, were attending to Andrea and Elsie in the first room that John entered. Both had intravenous drips running. Bill's eyes blazed fire when he saw John. Stepping away from the beds he approached him and snapped "Would you care to tell me what the hell is going on around here?"

"How are they?" asked John, looking first at Andrea Eagle. Her sweating face had a tortured, frightened expression and it was obvious that she was experiencing severe chest pain with every breath. John took her hand and tried to reassure her. Elsie Sims, the young nurse who had helped John with the Williams boy, coughed and choked repeatedly, producing copious amounts of mucus, and then fell back exhausted after each paroxysm, mumbling incoherently in her delerium of fever.

"John, I don't understand what's happening," complained Bill bitterly. "Three of our nurses and a lab tech down at the same time with some acute infectious process. They're all running high temps, they're all short of breath and coughing, and two of them have rales. The white counts aren't much help—two are in the 12,000 range and the other two are above 20,000. I can only assume we're dealing with the same disease. Emma is in the worst shape—she's cyanotic and almost totally unresponsive. I've never seen anything like this."

Before John could reply, Bill pointed a finger at him. "I know something strange is going on and I think you have some of the answers. Doug Harris tells me you sent Emma and Lee in from their homes. How did you happen to be making housecalls on staff? Also, Oliver's been running around with his head more up his ass than usual, acting like a kid that put his hand in the cookie jar and doesn't want to 'fess up."

"Bill, let's go into the doctors' lounge for a minute so we can talk in private." The two men left the room and removed their protective coverings, then walked down the corridor to the small lounge. After they entered John walked to the window and Bill came up alongside him. They looked down on Gallup's brown hills and the flat expanse of surrounding countryside, shielding their eyes from the glare of the sun, which had already begun its slow descent into the western desert.

"Bill, do you remember that sick Indian kid, Joseph Williams, who was pulled off the Peds service by his grandmother earlier this week?"

Bill nodded. "What does that have to do with anything?"

"The cultures of the boy's blood and sputum revealed plague bacillus."

Bill looked at him incredulously, his eyes bulging. "You've got to be shitting me."

John shook his head. "I wish I was. But Vincent is sure. The boy must have gotten the bubonic variety and progressed into a secondary plague pneumonia."

"Then all these people have pneumonic plague? Oh my God, John, do you know what this means? How long have you known this?"

"I just found out this morning. Then I checked with personnel to find out if anyone was out sick. And that's how I ended up sending Emma and Lee to the hospital. I know how serious this is but let's keep our heads and try to avert a panic. The cultures have all been taken on the four admissions?"

"All the lab work's been done except for X-rays."

"Then we'd better start treating them all with Streptomycin right away. And we've got to put all contacts on prophylaxis with Tetracycline. I'll talk to Pharmacy on that. And the families of the patients have to be quarantined at home and checked on every day. I've already taken care of that with Emma's sister and Lee's family and I'll bring some Tetracycline out to them. Can you take care of it with the families of the last two?"

"Andrea's husband and Elsie's brother are waiting outside. I'll arrange antibiotics and quarantine with them."

"We should set up a meeting for all medical staff, nursing supervisors and department heads and let them know what's happening. That will help us get everyone on prophylaxis. Is eight o'clock in the library okay?"

"That's fine with me."

John walked to the phone and called Oliver's office. He asked the secretary to set up the meeting and to have the telephone operator make an announcement.

"If the newspapers get hold of this," said Bill, "there's going to be mass hysteria. Unless we can get this under control, we may be up to our eyeballs soon in a full-blown epidemic."

"I know. We've just got to do what we can and try to play this down and impress on everyone how important—"

The lounge door swung open and Stuart Hollander, one of the internists, barged into the room. "Bill, "he said excitedly, "Emma Hastings just expired. She went into shock and we couldn't pull her out of it."

Bill frowned. "Did you say something about playing this down, John?"

"We still have to try to prevent a panic situation. I'll call Emma's sister and break the news. While you get the Streptomycin started, Bill, I'll contact Ralph Germain and ask him to do a post today. We might as well start corroborating what we think we know."

"Would someone care to enlighten me," said Hollander, looking from one to the other.

"I'll let Bill tell you and Jeff all about it. I'm heading down to see Tom Whitman, Bill. He's trying to locate the family of the Williams boy so we can trace contacts on that end. I'll see you at eight in the library."

"You know," called Bill, as John started to leave the lounge, "I don't know whether or not you've thought about it, but there are two other potential problems."

"What are they?"

"Us."

"I feel fine," smiled John. "Don't you?"

"I did until five minutes ago."

"Don't think about it. But we'd better start our Tetracycline anyway."

John hurried over to the Social Service office and then waited impatiently for Tom Whitman, who had apparently stepped out. Not more than two minutes had gone by when Tom entered and said simultaneously with John, "Oh, there you are." The tension was obvious on John's face and the laugh that ordinarily would have followed did not occur.

Tom pulled a paper out of his shirt pocket. "I was just over at Oliver's office to see if you'd gotten back. I think I've got the information you're looking for."

"Great. What did you find out?"

"Mary Begay and the boy live with Mary's son, Hosteen Williams, just this side of Twin Lakes. The boy's parents apparently work up in Shiprock. A Sing is being held for the boy in Tohatchi. It started yesterday and is still going."

"Incredible!" exclaimed John. "That means the boy is still alive." He looked at his watch. "If I leave right now I should be able to get to Tohatchi before six. Then the problem will be to find where the Sing is being held."

"Well, since I know Sam Begay, the Singer in Tohatchi," said Tom, "why don't I go along with you?"

"That would be great, Tom. I'd really appreciate it. You've been a fantastic help already. I don't know how the hell you came up with the information so quickly."

"I've got some good sources," smiled Tom.

"You sound like a reporter."

Tom laughed. "One that's in the dark. I'd still like to know what all this is about. Is it still top secret?"

"We're setting up a meeting for doctors and supervisors at eight tonight to talk about it but I might as well fill you in now. We think the Williams boy has plague."

"Bubonic plague?"

John nodded. "What makes it worse is that the infection was in his lungs, making him contagious as hell. Four of the staff have already come down with what we think is primary plague pneumonia, pneumonic plague. One of them, Emma Hastings, just died."

"Oh, John, that's terrible."

"We're putting everyone who came in contact with the boy on antibiotics. But now I need to know how many in the boy's family have been in contact with him. They'll need antibiotics, too, and we'll have to quarantine those who were exposed."

Tom tugged thoughtfully at his beard. "John, have you ever been to a Sing?"

"No. I've done some reading on traditional Navajo medicine but I've never seen one."

"You know that hundreds of people are sometimes in attendance."

John sighed in exasperation and shook his head. "We'll just have to hope that this one wasn't that well attended."

"I can tell you right now that if it's been going on since yesterday it's been very well attended."

"Then it looks like we have our work cut out for us. Once we get everyone on antibiotics we'll have one advantage on the reservation. The hogans are widely scattered so if we can discourage visiting and trips into Gallup, a mass outbreak would be unlikely."

"Unless, of course," cautioned Tom, "additional Sings are held for new cases."

"I hope the Singer will appreciate the problem and be willing to suspend his practice for a while."

"Sam Begay isn't the only Singer in this part of the reservation. But I do think he'll try to help us."

"In that case, Tom, I'll depend on your powers of persuasion. I'm going to stop by and see Oliver to let him know we're going. We should be back in time for the eight o'clock meeting, right?"

Tom nodded.

"Okay. Meet you in the parking lot in ten minutes. Oh, incidentally, Tom, if we have time on the way back I'd like to stop by and see Emma Hastings' sister. I have to drop off her Tetracycline and also, she doesn't know yet about Emma. Would you mind coming with me?"

"Not at all."

Walking back to the Administration Office, John felt relieved that Tom Whitman would be accompanying him to Tohatchi. It was going to be very difficult to explain the situation to the Indians and get them to comply with the antibiotic prophylaxis. Even more difficult would be the setting up of effective surveillance and obtaining the cooperation of the Singers on the reservation. He would have to depend heavily on the trust the Navajos placed in Tom.

CHAPTER 6 _____

THE FLAMING RED DISC OF THE SUN WAS SUSPENDED in the sky ahead of them as they drove up to Sam Begay's hogan. To the east the mesas were enveloped in a mauve afterglow and those families living in the Red Willow Valley had already seen the end of the sun for another day.

There were at least twenty vehicles parked around the hogan and scattered campfires were burning in preparation for the evening meal. Small clusters of men and women turned to watch the approach of the Anglos. They immediately recognized the giant with the blond beard but the shorter, darker one was unknown to most of them.

The door of the hogan opened and revealed the spare figure of Harvey Running Bear. After two nights with little sleep he looked more gaunt and haggard than usual and John knew that he was looking at a Navajo mystic, an Indian John the Baptist. That impression was strengthened by the chants of the Singer issuing from within the hogan. The coarse rhythms reverberated in the air around them. Running Bear recognized Tom Whitman and extended his hand. He indicated that they should pass into the hogan, and unobtrusively as possible they insinuated themselves into the outer fringe of the people who now occupied almost every square inch of the domed structure. Most of those further to the front were sitting so that the view of those standing in the rear was not obstructed.

To one side of the gasoline drum stove they could see the naked figure of Joseph Williams reclining on a sandpainting with Sam Begay standing over him and intoning the words of his chant. Two of the Singer's assistants, who were kneeling at the boy's side, then gently lifted Joseph Williams's inert form and removed him from the sandpainting. In the flickering glow of the kerosene lamps the few areas of the boy's body that were not thickly smeared with coal dust stood out in bold relief and John Hartman had the sinking feeling that his former patient was now indeed in the final throes of the "Black Death." He refused to even speculate on the number of people in the room now potentially at risk of becoming infected.

A few of the onlookers in the front circle suddenly stood up and approached the sandpainting. John recognized Mary Begay, the first woman to emerge from the group of women clustered at the north end of the hogan. She was followed by a younger woman. Several men also approached the painting and one of them, in response to the bidding of the Singer, walked across the pattern. He was followed in turn by each of the men and then by Mary Begay and the other women.

"Those men are probably the boy's father and uncles," whispered Tom. "The younger woman must be his mother."

"The older one is his grandmother, Mary Begay," replied John. "She's the one who took him out of the hospital. Why are they all stepping on the painting?"

"They're treading where the Holy People have walked. It puts the whole family into a close relationship with the holy figures."

Sam Begay now knelt next to Joseph Williams and lifted his head. He held a cup to the boy's mouth but John couldn't see if the boy was able to drink. The white-haired Singer then reached into his medicine bundle and began tying shiny bead-like objects to the boy's hair.

"Those turquoise pieces are so that the Holy People will recognize the boy as one of their own," explained Tom.

The Singer then resumed his chanting and took his feather stick to initiate the destruction of the sandpainting, beginning once again in the center of the painting and progressing toward the periphery.

"It seems a shame to destroy it," whispered John. "It's beautiful."

"It's absorbed all the evils," replied Tom. "The sand will be carried out to the north of the hogan and buried."

Although from within the confines of the hogan none of them could see outside, Sam Begay knew that the sun had begun its descent into the earth. The last traces of the drypainting had now been obliterated and one of the Singer's assistants began to sweep up the sand while Sam Begay again approached Joseph Williams and began his final chant of the day. It was the same one he used to end each day's ceremony, the "House Made of Dawn" prayer that ended with the lines, "May it be beautiful all around me. In beauty it is finished, in beauty it is finished."

With the conclusion of the chant, people began filing out of the hogan. The women resumed the task of cooking mutton and preparing frybread.

John stood transfixed, his mind still filled with the images he had witnessed. None of his reading about Dineh, "the people", and their centuries-old healing rituals had prepared him for the feelings he had experienced as an observer at the Sing.

"Impressive, isn't it?" asked Tom, but John didn't answer.

"It's too bad we came in on the tail-end. This was the Windways chant and it's a beautiful ceremony."

Gradually, John again became aware of the activity around him. People pressed by to join the throng at the mutton tub. Those who had received their fresh slabs of frybread reached into the tub to scoop up the mutton chunks, then made way for those behind them. John shook his head, as if trying to rouse himself from sleep, and looked at Tom. "I was really caught up in it at the end," he said, feeling a bit sheepish.

Tom laughed. "So I noticed."

"I'd like to see the boy now and talk to the Singer."

"Okay. Come on and I'll introduce you to Sam Begay."

The Singer sat by himself next to the stove, the exhaustion engendered by the first two days of the Sing evident on his lined face. He smiled when he saw Tom Whitman and they touched hands.

"Forgive me if I do not rise," he said. "Tonight I am feeling the weight of my years. It has been a difficult struggle."

"How is the boy, hatali?"

"He seems to be improved, but we will have to wait a while longer to see. I think that he will again walk in beauty."

"Hatali, this is Dr. Hartman from the Indian Health Center in Gallup. Dr. Hartman saw the boy in the hospital before his grandmother brought him to you for the Sing."

John extended his hand to the Singer and they touched palms.

"Sir, when the boy was brought in he was very ill. We thought at that time he had a serious infection in his lungs but before we could treat him Mary Begay took him out of the hospital. When the boy had been gone for a few days, we received a report from our laboratory that revealed the boy's infection was even more serious than we had thought, not only for him but for anyone who comes in contact with him because it is very contagious.

"Four of the people who helped care for Joseph Williams in the hospital have already contracted the disease and one of them, a nurse, died today." Sam Begay made no comment as John spoke. His face remained impassive and his gaze appeared to be focused inward but John knew that he was listening.

"We have a medicine that will offer some protection against the disease. Our people working in the hospital will take it and everyone on the reservation who has been in contact with Joseph Williams should also take it.

"For those who already have the germs in their system, the medicine will not be strong enough. I would like to warn everyone here about the symptoms of the disease so that at the first sign they will come to us for treatment. Without treatment, most people who get the disease will surely die."

At this point Tom broke into the conversation. "Hatali, Dr. Hartman believes as I do, that the medicine of Dineh is as strong as the white man's medicine. This disease called plague is so evil that it will need the strongest medicine of both of our peoples. One of the problems is that if someone has the disease and other people are near him, they may come down with the disease, too, because the germs are passed from sick people to healthy people. And so, hatali, we would like for anyone who has the disease to come to the hospital first. It will enable the doctors to treat the disease and keep the sick person away from others until he is well."

The Singer looked at Tom. "And how will harmony be restored without following The Way?"

"We are not asking that the sick ones be kept from following The Way, hatali. Only that we be allowed in these cases to give our treatment first. Then they can have the Sing when they've left the hospital."

"It will be difficult to persuade my people of this."

"I know, hatali. That is why we come to you for your help. We know you are respected by your people and that they will listen to you.

"Dr. Hartman would also like to examine Joseph Williams and then, with your permission, we would like to talk to everyone here."

Sam Begay looked at John, then turned to locate Mary Begay. She was sitting only a few yards from her grandson. The Singer rose slowly from the ground and approached her. They spoke for several moments and then Sam Begay indicated that John should join them.

"She says that you may examine the boy."

John looked down at the youth and was surprised to have his gaze met by the boy's. He kneeled and placed his hand on the boy's coal dust-smeared forehead. John guessed that there was still some fever present but it certainly was not as high as when he first saw Joseph Williams in the hospital.

'How do you feel, John?" he asked.

"Very tired," replied the boy weakly.

John felt the boy's pulse and found it to be just under 100. Although he was still breathing rapidly there was no obvious respiratory difficulty. Removing the stethoscope from his jacket pocket, John listened to the boy's chest. The breath sounds were coarse in some areas and there were still some rales in the lung bases but there was no doubt that the boy was distinctly improved.

"Joseph, do you remember handling any small animals before you got sick? A squirrel or a mouse or something like that?"

"My dog brings me animals sometimes. Just before I got sick he brought me a dead chipmunk."

"Do you remember having any bug bites on you after that?"

"I had some red pimples on my arms. I thought they were from ants."

John rose and looked intently at the Singer. The old man met his gaze.

"He's certainly much better than when I first saw him. Your medicine is very strong, hatali."

The old man did not reply. John hoped that the Singer was aware of the respect that the Anglo doctor felt for him.

"I believe that he still has traces of the infection in his lungs and I would like to treat him with some of my medicine in the hospital for a few days."

Sam Begay relayed this information to the boy's grandmother, who nodded and replied, looking at him as she spoke in Navajo.

"She says that when the Sing is over, the day that follows tomorrow, the boy may be put in your care and she is grateful for any help you can give. She also says that she would like to return this to you." The Singer took a folded grey hospital blanket handed to him by Mary Begay and gave it to John.

"I think that's the best you're going to do, John," said Tom Whitman. "Once her grandson is restored to the harmony of the Navajo Way, she'll let you have him."

John removed a bottle of Tetracycline capsules from his pocket and extended them toward the Singer. "Would you ask her, hatali, if she would be willing for the boy to begin taking this medicine now. He will have to take one four times a day for ten days."

The Singer spoke to Mary Begay and she nodded her agreement.

John smiled at Joseph Williams. "You're going to be fine, Joseph. After the Sing you'll be with us in the hospital for a few days so we can help make you strong again. It shouldn't be too difficult now that the Hatali has helped you so much."

The Singer walked over to Tom Whitman and placed his hand on his shoulder. "Your friend seems to care for our people and our ways."

"He does, hatali. He's a good person."

"I will arrange now for him to address our guests."

John rejoined Tom after the old man walked away. "It's hard to believe, Tom."

"What is?"

"It's a miracle. The boy is still sick but much better than he was in the hospital. I didn't think then that he had a prayer. I know he had one dose of Tetracycline but I didn't think it was possible for anyone to recover from plague pneumonia without intensive treatment."

"But he did receive treatment, John."

"You know what I mean. It wasn't exactly the treatment we'd equate with modern medical practice."

Tom smiled. "It's a good thing that you and I appreciate healing methods that complement one another."

"Anyway, I'll feel better now that the boy will be on Tetracycline until we get him in the hospital."

"Sam Begay is arranging for you to address everyone now.

"Will you join me, Tom? I think they'd accept what I'm going to say better if you were there to back me up."

"Sure, but don't forget that even with Sam Begay translating for you some things are going to be very difficult to get across. Navajo is a language of hunters and herdsmen, not scientists. There are some concepts that the Navajos don't undertstand and won't accept. But I do think that Sam Begay will help—even though he may not entirely agree with our way of handling things. He'll do it because he knows we're sincere and care what happens to his people."

The hogan had gradually begun to empty. People carried their food with them and and congregated near the campfires in front of the dwelling. Sam Begay returned to where John and Tom were standing and indicated that all was ready. John took one last look at Joseph Williams, who was now being dressed by Mary Begay, and followed the Singer from the hogan.

The sun had dropped below the mesas to the west and its rich orange glow filled the sky. The moon was already visible and the temperature had dropped by twenty degrees since John and Tom had first entered the hogan. The Indians clustered close to the fires and many had blankets draped over their shoulders.

John watched the faces of the gathering as the Singer began to speak. In the glare of the dancing flames, their features took on a primitive cast, a deceptive hardness that belied the gentle nature of a pastoral people. By giving free rein to his imagination, John could easily have believed that he had returned to a past that was in reality not too distant when the redmen met to discuss their strategy before confronting a common enemy. Only this time the enemy was an invisible one, one more menacing perhaps than the early white settlers who overran their lands.

John knew that the Navajos could deal with a visible enemy. They had had long experience in the art of survival and if their methods were at times self-defeating, they had at least survived, a claim that many tribes could not make. But to convince them that an unseen enemy was in their midst would require a major effort.

Sam Begay had stopped speaking and stood now looking at John. "You're on stage," whispered Tom.

John stepped forward and moved to the Singer's side. He hesitated for a moment to formulate his thoughts, then began.

"You all know that Joseph Williams has been very sick. He was in the hospital for a short time before being brought here for the Sing. After he left the hospital, four of the people who helped care for him became sick with the same disease Joseph has and one of them, a nurse, died this afternoon.

"The disease that Joseph Williams has is called plague. It's caused by bacteria carried by an insect, a flea, from small animals—squirrels, mice, chipmunks. These bacteria can only be seen under a microscope."

He spoke slowly, allowing ample time between sentences for Sam Begay to translate for those who did not speak English. John assumed that many of the older people still spoke only Navajo, and he observed that it was mainly they who looked at one another, unable to comprehend the existence of bacteria, invisible microscopic creatures that make one ill.

"Plague is a disease that has afflicted mankind for centuries," he continued. "It came to Egypt more than a thousand years ago and spread throughout Asia and Europe, killing more than a hundred million people. Then, about six hundred years ago, in a time we call the Middle Ages, the plague returned to Europe. Fleas that lived on infected rats attacked the people and gave the disease to them. Plague caused a high fever and a swelling of the glands in the body and, in some cases, attacked the lungs. The coughing then spread the disease to other people. This type of plague was even worse than the type given to people by the fleas. In those days there was no medicine for the plague and almost everyone who got the disease died. Twenty-five million people died in Europe alone. It was called the 'Black Death'.

"About a hundred years ago, the plague came to this country. It was probably carried in by rats on ships that came to San Francisco. In America, plague attacked small wild animals, the prairie dogs and squirrels and field mice. Since these animals don't live in people's houses, not many cases occurred here. But every year there are a few. When someone handles an animal that has the disease and the fleas on that animal bite the person, then the disease will come. That's what happened to Joseph Williams. His dog brought him a dead chipmunk and that chipmunk had the plague. The fleas on the chipmunk bit Joseph and he became sick. Even worse, the disease spread to Joseph's lungs and anyone who came in contact with him was at risk of getting the disease. That's why the nurses in the hospital got it."

There was a subdued mumbling among the people and it was obvious to John that his story was being received with skepticism, especially by the older people. The Navajos had listened respectfully, probably enjoying the narrative, but many did not believe what was being told to them.

From the assembly, a stocky man wearing a stetson stepped forward. He looked at John, then spoke in English.

"If people die from this disease, why hasn't Joseph Williams died? If, as you say, he gave the disease to the nurses and one of them has died, why is Joseph Williams still living?"

John tried to choose his words carefully before answering. "It isn't always possible to know all the answers. Joseph Williams did receive some antibiotics before his grandmother took him out of the hospital. That may have helped. Also, it is because God wanted him to live, and with the help of the hatali, he has.

"But the important thing is that most people who get the disease will die from it unless they get treated immediately."

"Then the hatali can help us," replied the same man, "if one of us gets the disease."

John sensed now that his mission had failed. In his frustration he turned to look at Tom.

"I'll give it a try if you want, John."

John nodded.

There was a general sound of approval as Tom Whitman prepared to speak. Most of those present knew the tall Anglo with the yellow beard and they obviously liked him.

"We all know that the hatali's medicine is very strong. But the plague, the disease that Dr. Hartman has told you about, is also very strong. Our best hope of overcoming it is by our working together, using the medicine of the white man and the medicine of the hatali. There's one medicine that we have in the Indian Hospital that we'd like to give to everyone who has been near Joseph Williams. It can prevent the disease or make it less severe if it occurs. Everyone who has been to this Sing should get the medicine."

He turned to John. "How about tomorrow morning?"

"That'd be fine. I'll have the hospital pharmacist stockpile additional Tetracycline and we'll contact the pharmacies in town to make sure they have enough on hand."

Tom spoke again to the crowd. "If you come to the clinic of the Indian Hospital tomorrow, we will give you the medicine.

"People who do get the disease will have fever and cough and be very sick. They should go to the hospital immediately because the sooner that treatment is given, the better the chances of recovery."

At this point, he was interrupted by the man in the stetson, who had apparently assumed the role of spokesman for the group.

"Why shouldn't we see the hatali instead of going to the hospital? You yourself said the medicine of the hatali is strong."

"I didn't say you shouldn't see the hatali. What I do say is that if you get the disease you should see the hatali after you have received treatment in the hospital. The reason for this is that the disease is so contagious. There are many people at a Sing and if they're near the sick person they can get the disease, too. Then we'll have many sick people instead of a few. If a sick person comes to the hospital for treatment, we'll give him strong medicine and as soon as he's better, he can see the hatali for the Sing."

The man in the stetson turned to those surrounding him and began speaking in Navajo. John could see that the people remained unconvinced.

It was then that Sam Begay intervened. As soon as he began to speak, the crowd fell silent. He spoke in a soft voice and everyone listened intently. In the distance, John heard the mournful wail of a coyote.

Following the hatali's words to the group, there was a short exchange between the man in the stetson and the Singer and then for the first time, Sam Begay raised his voice. The man fell silent and did not speak again.

Sam Begay now faced John and Tom. "I have advised them to go to the hospital for their medicine tomorrow and to tell all those who were here earlier that they, too, should receive the medicine.

"I have also told them that I will not conduct a Sing for anyone with this disease until they have been treated first in the hospital."

Both John and Tom were aware of how difficult this had been for the Singer. Believing as they did in the importance of using both Anglo and Navajo healers in a cooperative manner that would preserve the essentials of both "Ways", they appreciated the problem implicit in trying to maintain the spiritual influence of the hatali while at the same time they took away from him primary responsibility for managing the disease.

"Thank you, hatali," said John, feeling how totally inadequate his words were.

"We appreciate everything you've done," echoed Tom, his manner also subdued.

The hatali did not reply. He walked slowly back to the hogan, the usual vitality absent from his steps. John wondered if he was simply exhausted from the rigors of the Sing or if his decision to support the Anglo request, which, in effect, amounted to a relinquishing of his own authority, had sapped his strength.

"Well, Tom," said John, his voice betraying the emotions evoked by the Singer's gesture, "I guess we've accomplished what we came for. Tomorrow we'll know if the Singer's words influenced them. There is one thing that surprises me. Not one of them has come down with the plague after contact with the boy for the past few days."

"How long is the incubation period for the disease?"

"Usually one to three days for pneumonic plague."

"It is strange. Anyway, what did you think of Sam Begay?"

"He's quite a man. I think what he did required a great deal of courage."

"I agree with you. How many Anglos would be willing to subordinate their own interests for the common good? And you know, the hatali made his decision not because he believes we're right but because he believes we're sincere and he trusts us. As you say, he's quite a man."

Just then, Sam Begay emerged from the hogan and called to Tom. "Please bring the doctor here."

John and Tom looked at one another. "Oh, Christ, I hope the kid hasn't gone sour," said John, walking quickly toward the hogan.

"Mary is unconscious," said the Singer, as they came up to him.

John entered the hogan and saw the woman stretched out on the ground near Joseph Williams. The boy, now completely dressed, was lying on one side, his arm reaching out toward his grandmother.

"She won't get up," he whimpered when he saw John.

John felt the heat being given off by the woman's body as he lifted her wrist. Her pulse was rapid, at least 140 per minute, and judging by touch alone, he guessed she had a fever of 103 or higher.

"It looks like we have another patient," he said as Tom entered the room.

The boy began to cry and John patted his shoulder. "Don't worry, son, we'll take good care of your grandmother and she'll be fine. Now when you come to the hospital, your grandmother will be there with you."

Sam Begay stood at the entrance to the hogan and watched John. "Does she have the sickness?" he asked.

"It's not possible to say for sure yet, hatali, but she does have a high fever and since she's been with Joseph for a few days, I would have to say that it's probably plague. We'll take her to the hospital with us and start treating her right away."

"It is a bad disease," said the Singer, the pain of awareness very real on his face.

"Yes, hatali," said John, "it is. I thank you again for what you did tonight."

Sam Begay's expression did not change but his embarrassment was evident as he turned abruptly and left the hogan. Tom followed him and saw him approach the group of people still remaining outside. The Singer spoke in Navajo and pointed to the hogan. His words obviously had a profound effect on the people, for they looked alternatively at one another and at the hogan, and Tom was certain he detected fear on their faces.

Two of the men followed Sam Begay back to the hogan. "This is Hosteen and this is Buck," Sam said to Tom. "They are two of Mary's sons. They will help you to get Mary to the hospital." He then looked at the two Navajo men. "And you had better take the boy, Joseph, too."

"Thank you, hatali," said Tom. "We can put Mary on the back seat of our car and they can bring Joseph in their vehicle."

Mary's sons placed her on a blanket and carried her out to John's Ford. They then carried Joseph Williams to their pickup truck and placed him between the two of them. The Indians still at the campfire watched silently.

"We'll take good care of them, hatali," said John, as he started his car.

"I know you will," Sam Begay replied. "Tell Mary that when she leaves the hospital I will help her to walk in beauty once more."

"I will, hatali." He touched the Singer's hand and this time their palms remained in contact for several moments.

"Well," said Tom, as they drove away, "we may not have convinced them but Sam Begay and Mary probably did. I have a feeling you'll be seeing a lot of patients at the clinic tomorrow."

John watched the campfires fade away and then there were only the headlights of Hosteen's truck behind him. "I suppose it's fortuitous in a way that Mary came down with it when she did, but it really worries me. All those people in contact! It's a potential disaster."

They rode in silence for a quarter of an hour, each one deeply involved in his own thoughts. John knew that if a full-scale outbreak occurred, it would mean converting the entire hospital into one big communicable disease unit, which, in effect, would restrict, if not eliminate entirely, all other admissions. Provisional arrangements would have to be made with the smaller Indian Health Centers scattered through the reservation for the care of other patients. Then there was the problem of Gallup itself. With several staff members at the hospital already stricken by the disease there was always the possibility of transmission to the town's population no matter how stringent the quarantine measures. Calvary Hospital and the physicians of Gallup would have to be alerted. And as unhappy as it would make Russell Oliver, the people of Gallup would have to be apprised of the situation and told what symptoms to watch for.

A pickup truck roared by in the opposite direction and in the glare of its headlights John stole a glance at his watch. "We should make it back just in time for the conference," he said to Tom. "After it's over I'll bring the Tetracycline to Lee's family and Emma's sister. I hate breaking the news to Emma's sister over the phone so I'll tell her while I'm there."

"I can drive over there, John, if you'd like me to."

"That's good of you, Tom, but I feel I should be the one to tell her. If you don't mind though, I'll give you the Medina address and enough Tetracycline for Lee's mother and sister and you can bring it to them. That would be a big help."

"No problem. Anything else Social Services can help with?"

"Yes. The families who are in quarantine will need help with food shopping, discussing the situation with employers, that sort of thing. To be on the safe side, the quarantine for each family involved should last five days. Someone at the hospital should also check with them each day to make sure no one has developed any symptoms."

"Leave all that to me."

It was shortly before eight when they drove up to the Emergency entrance of the hospital. Hosteen's truck pulled up behind them. John found Doug Harris on duty and arranged for the admission of Mary Begay and Joseph Williams.

"Is it true we're dealing with plague, John?" Harris asked.

"I'm afraid so. These two go into isolation and respiratory quarantine just like the others."

"I'll be too busy to attend the meeting, John."

"We're just going to get the word to everyone and talk about antibiotic prophylaxis and precautions. Don't forget to start your Tetracycline. Which reminds me. I'd better start my own. I'll fill you in on anything else that comes up after the meeting's over. You'd better alert Bill Moore about the new admissions, too, so he can get help for you."

"Can't do it, John. Bill's sick, too. He called about an hour ago to say he had a fever and—holy shit! You don't suppose...!

The skin at the back of John's neck tingled the way it always did when he had a presentiment of things going badly. This was one of those times. "Where is he, Doug?"

"He said he was going off duty for a while and would try to get a little sleep in the doctor's lounge on three."

John raced up the stairs to the third floor and found Bill Moore stretched out on a sofa in the darkened lounge. He turned on a small lamp in one corner of the room, casting a long shadow on the wall as he approached Bill. In the dim light, Bill's usually florid face had a pasty yellow cast and there were deep shadows under his closed eyes. John gently touched his shoulder and Bill's lids fluttered, then opened slowly. For a moment he showed no sign of recognition, then smiled weakly. "That you, baby doc?"

"How are you feeling?" asked John, unable to mask his concern.

"Miserable. My head is splitting."

John reached down to touch his forehead and found what he expected. "You're burning up, Bill. When did the fever start?"

"It came on about midafternoon, at about the time I last saw you."

"I thought you were kidding when you said you didn't feel well."

"It was just a headache then. After you left I puked once. All my bones are aching, too. It might just be a gastroenteritis," he said hopefully.

"It might be but you know we can't take a chance. Not with what's going on all around us. It looks like you'll have to change roles for a while and act like a patient."

"Listen, John, if it was plague wouldn't you have it, too? You had as much contact with the kid as I did."

"To tell you the truth, Bill, I've been wondering why the hell I haven't come down with it yet. Maybe I'm so saturated with all the crud the kids cough and breathe on me every day that the bacillus can't get a foothold. Or maybe I'm just lucky—so far. But you still have to be admitted. Who knows? I might be in the bed next to you later."

"You're too ugly," replied Bill.

John laughed. "I'm heading down to the meeting in the library. I'll have hotshot Hollander make the arrangements for you and you can have him as your personal physician. Incidentally, you're not going to believe this but I found the boy, Joseph Williams."

"Where was he buried?"

"He wasn't. We found him at the Sing, still alive and it looks like he's recovering. His grandmother's got the bug though. Tom Whitman and I brought them both in and they're being admitted right now."

"John, maybe it's not plague. How the hell could the kid survive plague pneumonia without treatment?"

"We have to assume it's plague if the lab isolated the bacillus. The post on Emma Hastings will give us the definitive answer."

"Ralph Germain should be doing it right now. He told me he was going to start by seven."

"Okay. Look, I'd better get downstairs. Someone will be here in a few minutes to take you to the ward and I'll be up to see you later."

At the door, John paused and turned. "The kid did have his first dose of Tetracycline while he was here. And don't forget, the Singer treated him, too, for the past two days."

With an effort, Bill raised himself on his elbows. In that position his face was barely visible in the room's gloomy light. "Well, the hell with Stuart Hollander then. Bring me a fucking Singer!"

John had to smile at Bill's retort in spite of the worries that preoccupied him as he took the stairs down to the library. Things are going from bad to worse, he thought. Bill's illness would not only cause hardships on the medical service but it would be demoralizing for the rest of the hospital's staff.

"Oh, I'm glad you're back, John, called Russell Oliver, approaching the library as John appeared. "I was afraid you might not make it back in time for the meeting. Did you find the boy?"

"Yes. He was still alive, actually better, which is hard to believe. His grandmother's got it though so we're admitting both of them. And I'm afraid I have more bad news. Bill Moore is up in the third floor lounge with a high fever."

The administrator gasped. "John, you don't think..."

"I don't know but it's possible. He'll have to be admitted."

"Oh my God, this is getting entirely out of hand."

"You're telling me."

For several moments the two men looked helplessly at one another before John broke the silence. "We'd better go into the meeting. I've got to tell Stu Hollander about Bill and get him admitted. I understand, too, that Germain is doing the post on Emma Hastings right now. After the meeting I'll talk to him."

The library was filled when John and Oliver walked into the room. All the chairs at the long table were occupied and small groups congregated along the sides of the room. The buzz of conversation halted abruptly as they entered. It was difficult to tell from their faces whether or not they had already picked up any information about the nature of the problem. They were certainly aware of the rash of admissions among staff.

John called Stuart Hollander over and in a low voice told him about Bill Moore. Hollander left the room at once and John walked up to the podium. He immediately launched into a litany of events beginning with the admission of Joseph Williams. It was apparent that most of the physicians in the room had already been briefed. They remained attentive while others murmured audibly, stunned at the news of the outbreak and the swath it had cut through the staff. Their consternation increased when John informed them about Bill Moore's admission and they sat in shocked silence. At that moment, Doug Harris opened the door and stuck his head in. All heads turned toward him.

"Elsie Sims just passed away," he said.

Conversation erupted around the room and John was forced to pound on the podium to get everyone's attention. "Please—let me continue and then we can handle questions one at a time. We've got to remain calm and prevent a panic from spreading throughout the hospital.

"Everyone in the hospital who has had contact with an affected patient should begin taking Tetracycline. It can be picked up at the pharmacy and it should be taken for six days. The incubation period for the disease is three or four days max so if symptoms haven't developed by then, there's probably no danger. Respiratory precautions have got to be strict in patient rooms and you'll have to emphasize that to nursing and lab staff.

"Tomorrow we expect the Indians who have been in contact with the sick boy to begin arriving at the clinic at eight in the morning for their Tetracycline." He paused to look at the pharmacist, who was seated at the table. "Jerry, do we have enough Tetracycline for staff and for the Indians? I expect we could have as many as a hundred people showing up tomorrow."

The pharmacist gnawed on his thumb. "I know we've got enough for staff. I'll arrange an emergency shipment for tomorrow and I'll talk to the pharmacists in town to get more. I think we'll be okay in the short run."

"Families of those affected have to be kept in strict quarantine for four or five days," John continued. "I've got Tom Whitman working on that.

"With Bill Moore sick, the other internists will have their hands full but one of you should make up a description of plague symptoms and signs. Mr. Oliver's secretary can run off the copies and they should be distributed to everyone in the hospital. Inform your staffs that time is of the essence in treating this infection. Even a delay of several hours could make the difference between life and death. With early treatment with Streptomycin, the chance of a cure is excellent.

"I think, too, it would be best if we close off the entire medical floor and use it for treatment of plague patients only. We can transfer other medical patients to other floors. The nursing supervisors can consult with the physicians and arrange that.

"Above all, we've got to keep our heads. All the physicians in town will be notified and the people of Gallup are going to have to be told what we're up against. With staff members who live in town already infected, we have to make sure the infection doesn't spread and we have to avert a panic."

Russell Oliver sat morosely at the table and listened to John. With two nurses already dead and his chief of medicine probably infected, averting a panic, he thought, would verge on the impossible. He already felt sorry for himself. There was no telling when he would get back to the greens again. He just knew his putting game was going to be shot to hell.

When John left the library, he headed immediately for the autopsy room. Emma Hastings was still on the table, her chest and abdomen already closed up, and Ralph Germain, still gowned and masked, sat at a small desk, dictating his notes. He looked up as John approached and indicated a gown and a box of caps and masks near the door.

"What did you find, Ralph?" asked John, as he tied his mask.

"Pulmonary edema and a hydrothorax. A lot of small nodules in her lungs. Those will be sectioned and cultured."

"What do you think?"

"I won't know until I see the slides and get the culture reports."

"But don't you have an impression? Do you think it's plague?"

"Plague is a possibility."

John knew that was about the best he would get out of Ralph Germain for now. He was an excellent pathologist but slow about committing himself. If Ralph Germain looked at a globe he'd say it was probably round. If he said plague was a possibility, John knew that was the diagnosis he favored.

After leaving the laboratory, John remembered that he had forgotten to begin taking his Tetracycline and hadn't eaten anything since breakfast. He stopped at the pharmacy and picked up a five day supply, took his first one at the water fountain, and went to the coffee shop to get a sandwich.

Before leaving the hospital, he made chart rounds on the Pediatrics ward, then went up to the medical ward, where he found Stuart Hollander writing furiously in a chart at the nurses' station. Now that he has the chief of medicine as a patient, he'll be more unbearable than usual, thought John, smiling to himself.

"How is he doing?" John asked.

Stuart Hollander looked at him with the air of a man who wondered why pediatricians were necessary in this world. "He's sleeping."

"He's sleeping," John repeated. "Is that your summation of his condition?"

"The necessary blood work has been ordered and Streptomycin has been started." He continued writing as he spoke, then looked up with a toothy smile, as if to say, 'are you satisfied'?

"Keep up the good work," called John as he headed for the stairs. He knew that as wretched as Stuart was on a personal basis, his medical skills were of a high order. Stuart Hollander frowned as John left and wondered why the Indian Health Service didn't build separate pediatric hospitals. Children and their doctors were simply intolerable.

The cool night air was invigorating and John breathed deeply as he walked into the parking lot. It had been a very long day and it was not over yet. He still had to break the news to Emma Hastings' sister.

A shooting star flashed across the sky as he entered his car. Moments later there was no sign that it had ever existed. John stared at the spot where it had been and his eyes suddenly filled with tears. He wished that Beth were sitting next to him and that he could bury his face between her breasts.

CHAPTER 7

THE FOLLOWING EVENING JOHN HARTMAN DID NOT leave the hospital until almost seven. He had been on duty for twelve hours and his body ached with fatigue. If the previous day had been interminable, this day had been worse.

He had had only a few hours of fitful sleep. The visit to Emma Hastings' sister had been a painful experience with the woman taking the news very badly. It had been necessary to sedate her and then wait for her to fall asleep before he could leave. He also had to make certain that she would begin taking her Tetracycline. While waiting, he had called Lee Medina's house and reassured the family that she was doing well. And when, finally, he returned to his own apartment, his troubled thoughts had given him little rest. He brooded on the deaths that had occurred, people whom he had admired and whom he felt would be irreplaceable at the hospital. It was too soon to know how many more would be cut down by the disease before it ran its course. Tears and lamentation, he thought. Those words had suddenly come to him and they were appropriate, he knew, for there would be more to come.

He had already been awake for some time when he left for the hospital at six rather than spend another restless hour in bed. To his surprise, he found the clinic waiting room filled and many of the faces were familiar to him from the Sing. There were already almost a hundred Navajos present, occupying every available seat and lining the wall. His eyes met those of a man in the front row and he recognized Sam Begay. John smiled and approached the Singer.

"I'm glad you're here," he said. "We'll begin distributing the medicine as soon as the pharmacist gets here."

The old man nodded. "More will be coming," he said simply.

While the secretaries began processing the patients, John headed up to the medical ward to check on Bill Moore and the other affected patients.

It was no surprise to hear from the nurse on duty that all, except Joseph Williams, were still quite sick. Intramuscular Streptomycin in high doses, the drug of choice for plague, was being administered in every case and it appeared that everyone was at least holding his own. In contrast to the four adults, each of whom had a fever in the 104 range, young Joseph Williams' temperature was only slightly over 100 and he was requesting food on an hourly basis, a sure sign of his impending recovery.

John put on his gown, cap and mask and entered the room where Bill Moore had a bed to himself. The chief of medicine was only a few years older than John but his anxious, fever-ravaged face now gave him a much older appearance. An intravenous solution dripped slowly into one arm and he feebly raised the other in greeting.

"I know one thing, Bill," said John, trying to mask the concern he felt for his friend, "if I could get you on a tennis court right now I could probably take two sets out of three."

Bill's lips moved in reply but his attempt at speech was interrupted by a dry rasping cough. John patted his arm. "Plenty of time to argue with me later after the Streptomycin knocks off some of those bugs. Is hotshot taking care of you?"

Bill nodded. He twisted restlessly in the bed, seemingly unable to find a comfortable position. John had become cognizant now of two attributes of the disease that all the patients seemed to share—marked restlessness and an anxious facial expression. He had treated many acute infectious processes, both in adults and children, but seldom had he seen patients so toxic.

He left Bill's room and headed for his own ward to make rounds. Despite the presence of some acutely ill children in Pediatrics, mostly cases of infectious diarrhea and severe otitis, these problems seemed minor in comparison to what was happening on the medical ward. While completing the charting on his patients, he heard his name being paged.

The physician on duty in the Emergency Room was calling to inform John about the first patient on his shift. "I just thought you might like to know we have another case of what appears to be plague. The guy's name is Hosteen Williams—he's the son of the old lady you brought in from the reservation last night. He was sitting in the clinic with the other Indians when he got sick. Stu Hollander is down here with him now." There was silence for several moments on both ends of the line. "It's frightening, isn't it, John?"

"Very," replied John softly. "Keep me posted if any more cases come in on your shift."

Feeling more like an epidemiologist at this point than a pediatrician, John headed down to Social Services to see if Tom Whitman had arrived for work. He was not surprised to find him with papers spread out on his desk.

"Everyone at the Medina household all right last night?" John asked.

"They were fine. I gave them their Tetracycline and made sure they started taking it. I took mine this morning before breakfast. It's great on an empty stomach," Tom said, making a sour face. "I did some reading in the library last night after I left the Medinas. With what I know now about this fine disease, I think I'd take anything to prevent it, no matter how it made me feel."

John slumped in a chair next to Tom's desk and rested his chin on his fist.

"You look like you didn't sleep too well, buddy."

"I didn't."

"How's Bill Moore this morning?"

"Pretty sick. Hollander's taking care of him. I imagine we'll know better by tonight how he's responding to the Streptomycin. We just got a new admission—another case from the reservation. Mary Begay's son. He's the one who followed us in his truck last night with Joseph Williams."

Tom tapped his pencil thoughtfully. "Well, at least the Indians are coming to the hospital. I saw Sam Begay in the clinic this morning and it looked like he had brought half the reservation with him. Oh, by the way, don't worry about the families we have in quarantine. My people have been in phone contact with all of them and they won't lack for anything."

"Good. Thanks, Tom."

At that moment, John's name was announced over the paging system and Tom handed him the phone. He listened intently for a moment, then hung up.

"Oliver wants to see me."

Tom chuckled. "He's probably cursing up a storm. Imagine having a plague epidemic come along to ruin your golf game."

"I'll talk to you later, Tom."

"Okay. And listen—I know you don't know the difference between a bogey and a birdie, but try to console him." Tom's throaty laugh followed him out the door. John found the administrator pacing back and forth in his office.

"Good morning," John said, feeling the emptiness of the words.

"Good morning, my ass," replied Russell Oliver. "We've got big troubles, John. I've had my phone ringing since seven this morning. The mayor wants to see me. CDC wants all the details. BIA is sending some top brass down. I don't even have time to take a shit!"

"Well," said John, ignoring the tirade, "on the positive side the Indians are all coming in for their prophylaxis and the only two cases on the reservation so far, besides the boy, are the two family members who had closest contact with him. If we can shut it down on the reservation, we should be in pretty good shape."

"But what about in the hospital?"

"We've got strict precautions in effect on the ward and everyone who's had contact with patients is on Tetracycline. The next few days should tell the story."

The buzzer on Oliver's phone sounded. His face flushed as he listened. "Oh, shit. Send them in. I might as well get it over with.

"We have a little delegation," he said to John as he replaced the receiver. "The Mayor, Jason Oglethorpe, and Karl Stanhope."

"Would you like me to leave?"

"Hell, no! I'll need you to back me up and put a good spin on things—if you can find anything good to say. Besides, this will be an education for you."

Although John had never personally met any of the people Oliver named, he did not have to be told who they were. Oglethorpe was the owner of the largest trading post in town and, not surprisingly, was the real power broker in Gallup. His family was reputed to be the richest in the area. Hector Rivera, the mayor, had, in effect, been chosen by Oglethorpe and it was known that he took his orders directly from the trader. Karl Stanhope, the administrator of Calvary Hospital, was another member of Gallup's select circle and wielded his power like an old-time czar. John had heard the story of Seymour

Hirsch, a New Yorker who was his predecessor at the Indian Health Center and who had applied for privileges at Calvary with the intention of remaining in Gallup as a practitioner once his Indian Health Service stint was completed. He knew, of course, that Calvary was closed to any new doctor, especially to someone considered an "outsider". And in Hirsch's case, his qualifications as an outsider were indisputable—he was from New York, Jewish, and had worked in the "Indian Hilton".

Where Hirsch differed from those who had been rejected before him was in his refusal to take the rebuff lying down. He hired an attorney in Albuquerque and filed suit against Calvary for discriminatory practices. Within one week after the suit was filed, Hirsch was transferred from the Indian Health Service in Gallup to a field station in Montana, this in spite of having only two more months to serve. The word that filtered down was that Karl Stanhope had placed a call to Washington.

The three men filed in and shook hands very tentatively with Oliver. It looks like they're afraid of catching something, thought John. The administrator introduced John and this time the men merely nodded in a perfunctory way, no one proferring his hand.

The three were a study in contrasts—Rivera, a suave moustached Mexican, no more than forty, dressed in a powder blue suit with a bola tie; Oglethorpe, in his sixties, his skin deeply tanned, wearing a rancher's denim garb and carrying a stetson in his hand; and Stanhope, a somewhat rotund, outwardly jovial hail-fellow-well-met type of about fifty, whose eyes were a cold crystalline blue and gave the lie to his outward demeanor.

As soon as they were seated, Rivera and Stanhope deferred to Oglethorpe and the trader wasted no time in getting to the point.

"Mr. Oliver, we understand you have an epidemic of plague in your hospital—and also, that there have been cases on the reservation."

The administrator fidgeted nervously with some papers on his desk and cleared his throat. "I wouldn't term it an epidemic but it is true that we have had several cases."

"What does several mean?"

"There have been five cases among the staff and three from the reservation."

Karl Stanhope fixed Oliver with his icy stare. "And you don't consider that an epidemic?"

"I think what Mr. Oliver is trying to say," interrupted John, "is that this small outbreak hasn't reached epidemic proportions. And we're doing everything we can to make certain it doesn't."

Stanhope ignored John and looked at Oglethorpe. The trader turned his stetson slowly in his hands. "Mr. Oliver, this plague is quite serious from what I understand."

"Yes, it is."

"And I believe you have had deaths."

"Yes, two."

"You would agree then that we're dealing with a highly contagious, extremely lethal infection?"

Oliver shot a quick glance at John as if to ask where this line of questioning was leading.

"Yes, it is contagious and serious."

"Well, then, Mr. Oliver, I'm certain that you join us in our concern for the welfare of all the citizens of this town—and will assist us in every way in implementing the proposals we've drawn up."

Here it comes, thought John.

"What proposals are you referring to?" asked Oliver.

Rivera took a paper from his inside jacket pocket and unfolded it carefully. He smiled at Oliver and the gold lining of one incisor glistened.

"We propose," he read in his lilting English, "that Gallup be closed to all Indians from the reservation until an independent team of physicians decides the epidemic has ended. Checkpoints will be set up by the Highway Patrol to enforce this.

"We also propose that the staff and patients of this hospital be isolated from the town for the duration of the epidemic. Employees would either be quarantined in their homes or living quarters will be made available to them in the hospital."

"It would seem to me," interjected Stanhope, noting the stunned expressions of Oliver and John, "that you would not want to admit any other patients to the hospital while you're treating patients with plague. Any patients hospitalized at present who become ready for discharge can, of course, be returned to the reservation if that's where they live. What it boils down to is that you would need fewer staff."

"We also propose," continued Rivera, "that the Indian Health Service undertake an immunization program for all the citizens of Gallup.

"Also, that any new cases of plague, whether among Indians or the other citizens of Gallup, be treated in the Indian Health Center."

"It would be senseless to contaminate Calvary Hospital," interjected Oglethorpe.

Rivera folded up the paper and once again flashed his golden smile. Except for the buzzing of a fly on the window pane there was silence in the room. John had listened to the proposals in disbelief and looking now at Oliver's face, he saw that the administrator had been affected in the same way. John wondered if Oliver would even be able to regain his speech to reply.

The silence began to make the three visitors uncomfortable.

"Well?" asked Oglethorpe, directing the question to Oliver.

The administrator's color slowly returned and he flushed deeply, the way he usually did when excited or angry.

"Gentlemen, what you ask is impossible."

The three men looked at one another and then again at Oliver.

"Impossible?" asked Stanhope, his eyes now two small beads.

"You're asking in effect that we isolate the reservation from Gallup, suspend medical care to the Indians, lay off most of our staff and keep the others virtual prisoners."

"Come now," smiled Rivera, "there's no need to exaggerate. We're just trying to do what's in the best interest of the people of Gallup."

"If any new cases occur on the reservation, how do you propose that they receive medical care?" asked John.

"We have no objection to an ambulance making runs back and forth between here and the reservation. You could set up a pickup and drop-off point on the reservation for patients," replied Oglethorpe.

"What about other illnesses among the Indians—medical or surgical emergencies, for instance? If we lay off staff and limit ourselves only to plague cases, where will they receive care? Will Calvary take them?" asked John, directing the question to Stanhope.

"Now, doctor," replied the administrator of Calvary in a condescending manner, "you know we're a private hospital for the people of Gallup and that we don't accept patients from the reservation. The Indians can go to Shiprock."

"It's a long way to Shiprock when you have an acute appendix or a woman in labor," persisted John.

"For a man of science, you certainly can be melodramatic, doctor," smiled Stanhope, his manner seemingly affable but his eyes revealing something very different. "The Navajos are used to hardships. Besides, they'd rather see their own healers anyway."

John experienced a feeling of revulsion at having to carry on a dialogue with a man for whom he felt nothing but contempt. Before he could reply, Russell Oliver interrupted.

"Aren't you all concerned about the effect it would have on the commerce of the town if the Indians weren't permitted to come in from the reservation? Surely, Mr. Oglethorpe, you above all must appreciate that."

"Of course we've taken that into consideration, Mr. Oliver. And it's true that my own business would suffer. But this is no time for personal considerations—we have to think of the common good."

"Well, gentlemen, what you're asking of me is not within my power to grant. We're expecting a high level delegation from BIA and it would have to be their decision whether or not to limit admissions and cut staff and services. The same goes for the provision of plague vaccine, which Dr. Hartman tells me is almost never used. Isn't that correct, John?"

"Yes. It only has short-term effectiveness, requires a series of shots, and also has uncomfortable side-effects. I'm sure your physicians at Calvary will tell you the same thing." He directed the last statement directly at Stanhope.

"Furthermore," continued Oliver, "until we receive authorization from BIA and IHS head office, no Anglo can be admitted here, plague or no plague."

"Isn't it true that you have already admitted Anglo patients with plague?" asked Stanhope, no longer smiling.

"Only staff people who have contracted the disease while caring for patients."

"Well, Mr. Oliver," asked Oglethorpe in his voice of reason, "don't you think that sounds discriminatory? If the Indians start an epidemic and Anglos in Gallup are affected, aren't those Anglos entitled to the same medical care as Anglos working in the hospital?"

"The Indians did not start an epidemic," retorted John sharply, trying to hold his temper in check. "And if you"re so concerned about the Anglos of Gallup, why not admit them to one section of Calvary for their treatment, just as we're doing? Or are you afraid that the other Anglos in town won't want to use the hospital if they know you're caring for plague patients?" This time John received a venomous glare from Stanhope, who turned to Oliver.

"We're not here to bargain with you," he said. "The authorities of this town have reached certain decisions and we expect that they'll be implemented."

"I've already told you that I don't have the authority," said Oliver, his face flushing deeply.

"Well, Mr. Oliver," said Oglethorpe abruptly, "it appears that we're at an impasse of sorts. But we do have some authority and at this very moment Sheriff Carter is setting up checkpoints. No Indian from the reservation will be permitted to enter Gallup. And I'm sure that when your BIA team arrives today they'll concur that our proposals are best for everyone. We had hoped to have your cooperation so that everything could be arranged more expeditiously but if we have to wait another few hours, so be it."

He stood up, put on his hat, and turned toward his companions. "Well, gentlemen, our business here is concluded for the time being."

Without another word to John or Oliver, the three men filed out of the office. As soon as the door was closed, Oliver brought his fist down on his desk, sending papers flying. "Those goddamn sons of bitches!" he bellowed.

"Sir, is it legal for them to block access into Gallup from the reservation?"

"Nothing is legal where those bastards are concerned! I"m going to call the U.S. attorney in Albuquerque to see if he'll intercede. And if he won't, then, by God, I'll call the Attorney General's office."

John's anger had slowly subsided, only to be replaced by perplexity. There were simply too many things that seemed to defy explanation—but he knew that one person would probably have the answers. Tom Whitman had been in Gallup long enough to know every aspect of town politics and Indian-Anglo affairs. If anyone could throw some light on what had transpired in the administrator's office, it would be Tom.

"Well, I'd better check to see how everything is going on the ward and in the clinic. I also want to call the families of our staff patients."

"All right, John, but keep me posted on everything and for God's sake, try not to find any more cases!"

John walked quickly over to Tom's office and found him still seated at his desk, gnawing on a pencil as he read through his reports.

"Back already?" he asked.

"You won't believe what happened, Tom—or maybe you will. Oliver had a visit from three of the most disagreeable people it's ever been my misfortune to meet—Oglethorpe, Stanhope and Rivera."

Tom frowned. "The unholy trio. What the hell did they want?"

John related the proposals that had been put forth, including in his narration the responses made by Oliver and himself. Tom twirled the eraser end of the pencil in his lips as he listened, then scratched his beard as John finished. It was obvious from the set of his jaw that he was troubled.

"What I can't understand," complained John, "is why Oglethorpe would want to stop the Indians from coming into Gallup. He's sure as hell not the altruistic type—and his business especially would be hurt by a move like that. Another thing that baffles me is how they know so much—they know what's going on in the hospital, how many cases have been admitted, even that an Anglo doctor had been admitted. They also knew that BIA officials were coming here for a visit today. It doesn't make sense."

"It all makes more sense than you think, buddy," responded Tom. "To answer your second question first, Oglethorpe knows everything that happens in this town—he should since he runs the place and has plenty of people on his payroll. Unofficially, of course. Including people in this hospital. They must have called him as soon as all this started. And I'd bet my last dollar that he or his pal, Stanhope, placed the call to BIA that led to their coming visit—and that doesn't bode well. Those two have too many connections in Washington and it wouldn't be the first time they've influenced Bureau policy in Gallup—collusion is an ugly word but a rose by any other name...

"Your first question, on the surface at least, appears tougher to answer—but all you'd need to know is a little history. The Oglethorpes have been in these parts for a long time—they know all the angles and it's made them rich. Nothing Oglethorpe or the others do is altruistic, I assure you. To begin with, the Navajos have been getting more conscious lately of how badly they've been duped and cheated by the traders for the last hundred years—they're talking collectives and Indian stores for the sale of their craftwork to tourists—and they're asking for a fairer price for their work from the traders. Closing the town to them would make them pretty hungry and pretty desperate after a while—Oglethorpe could then easily arrange to buy their goods at a much lower price and he would see that the rugs, jewelry, et cetera were brought from the reservation to Gallup. That wouldn't be difficult with Sheriff Carter's men manning the checkpoints. Oglethorpe has enough inventory to last him a long time, so a few weeks or even months, I'd imagine, wouldn't bother him—it would hurt some other traders, of course, but Oglethorpe might be willing to sell to them at a substantial profit once he began receiving the goods. He'd pretend that he's supplying them from his own stock and everyone would think he's a swell guy—and entitled to his profits. The other aspect is that Oglethorpe holds more pawn than any other trader—he's got a fortune in silver and turquoise jewelry— and the longer the Navajos could be kept out of Gallup, the more the unclaimed pawn. It all adds up to a nice fat profit for Mr. Oglethorpe.

"As far as the other businesses in Gallup are concerned, who would be affected most by keeping out the Indians from the reservation? The liquor stores and saloons, of course. And you'd think that they would bitch loudly. But they won't—because one of Mr. Oglethorpe's other sidelines is contraband. He's been arranging the smuggling of booze onto the reservation for years. That's one of the reasons some of the wiser heads on the Tribal Council are arguing for not keeping the reservation dry. They realize that the problem is education, not the booze itself—an Indian can always buy liquor, either in Gallup or the contraband on the reservation—at a stiff price, of course, which he's always willing to pay.

"Anyway, Mr. Oglethorpe would simply expand his smuggling operation and make sure that the liquor store and saloon owners were kept happy."

"What a filthy business!" exclaimed John.

"It's filthy all right and a way of life out here. It's free enterprise at its most sordid—and it will be a long time before it changes. The education process for the Navajo will be a slow one because the

Anglos are going to put every obstacle they can think of in the way.

"I think you guessed right incidentally on their demand that all plague patients be admitted to this hospital. It will ensure that Stanhope maintains maximum bed utilization in Calvary."

"You don't think that they'll be able to carry out their proposals, do you, Tom?"

"Well, my first inclination would be to say no—but knowing Oglethorpe gives me some pause. One ploy he could use, for example, is the newspapers. I haven't seen anything in the local rag but—"

"Oh, that reminds me," interrupted John. "Oliver said the reporters had been bugging him."

"That's probably at Oglethorpe's instigation. I have a feeling that the paper will give it a big front page spread and use scare tactics. That would stir the locals up enough to give Oglethorpe a solid base of support—not that he really needs it since he can ultimately get his way. But it would help to put pressure on in case they meet any resistance from BIA, for example."

"I simply can't see them getting away with closing access to Gallup for the reservation Navajos and setting up policy for an Indian Health Service hospital. Oliver is contacting the U.S. attorney in Albuquerque about the checkpoints being set up, and if the BIA visitors accede to Oglethorpe's demands for the hospital, I don't think even Oliver would take that without a fight."

"You never know, John. 'Don't make waves' is his motto. And it's difficult for me to conceive of him bucking his superiors—especially since he's close to retirement."

John fell silent and stared at the floor. He wondered if it was just fatigue that made him feel so depressed—or the awareness that everything seemed to no avail when measured against power and money.

The change that had come over him was quickly discerned by Tom. "Hey, buddy, don't give up yet—I said the picture was gloomy, not hopeless. Oglethorpe is powerful in these parts and he and Stanhope certainly have connections in Washington—but basically they're still smalltime tyrants—and they can be fought. Let's wait and see what happens before we make any moves." He laughed suddenly. "Besides, you have a friend in Washington who's certainly higher level than any hack they might know in BIA."

"Who's that?" asked John.

"The Secretary of State—Sam Spencer. I understand you and he spent some time together when he visited."

John was taken by surprise at the reference to Sam Spencer. It had been less than a week since he came to the hospital and yet John had completely forgotten about him. Nevertheless, it had been Sam Spencer who had precipitated the whole train of events by bringing Joseph Williams to the hospital.

"I'll bet he'd be surprised if he knew what was happening here," said Tom. "In a way he's responsible for the whole thing."

A thought suddenly struck John. "Hey, Tom, do you know that we never even contacted Spencer to advise him of what was going on. I mean, he was exposed to the boy and—"

"Oh, come on, John. If Sam Spencer was sick it would be all over the newspapers—especially now. There was a picture of him, just yesterday, I think, shaking hands with some highpowered folk. He's so involved with the coming peace talks he's probably forgotten already that he ever was in Gallup."

"But still, Tom, we should try to contact him. Just to be on the safe side. I'm going to put a call through to the State Department to see if I can reach him."

"Lots of luck, my friend. After you talk to Spencer, why don't you call the President and give him my regards."

"You idiot," laughed John.

"Well, anyway, it should be an interesting day. Let's meet later to go over everything and talk strategy. Say, what are you doing tonight? How would you like to head over to Manuelito with me? There's this great Mexican restaurant that a friend of mine, Senora Rios, just opened and I hear she's got the best chicken mole this side of the border."

John thought about the invitation and then suddenly realized he had a date with Beth for that evening. With everything that was happening even that had slipped his mind.

"I'd love to, Tom, but I'm tied up for tonight."

"Oh? And who's the unlucky lady?"

John smiled and shook his head. "Top secret."

"I'll bet," said Tom. "Probably some eight year old on Peds with long pigtails and chickenpox."

"Ask me again during the week though and I'll take you up on it.

I'll see you later today and let you know if I find out anything else."

After leaving Tom's office, John passed through the clinic area and saw the Indians lined up at the pharmacy window. As each received his supply of Tetracycline, he was handed a cup of water and asked to take his first dose right there.

John noticed Sam Begay on the line and waved, receiving in turn an almost imperceptible nod. It was difficult to believe that this nondescript old man was the same person he had seen the night before performing the Windways chant in the hogan in Tohatchi.

Once in his office, John called the families of each of the staff members who had contracted the disease. He was relieved to hear that no one had any symptoms of illness. So far, so good, he thought, as he placed his next call to the State Department in Washington.

The operator at State transferred his call and a secretary answered. John identified himself and told her it was important that he speak directly to Sam Spencer but she brushed aside his request rather curtly and asked for the details. John insisted on talking only to Spencer and the woman, her exasperation evident, transferred his call to another office.

"Undersecretary Dodson," said the voice at the other end.

Once again John made his request. "I'm sorry, doctor," replied the voice, "but the secretary is in conference and can't be disturbed under any circumstances. If you will leave your number with me, I'll see that he gets the message."

Realizing he had no chance of speaking directly to Spencer and not wishing to divulge the fact that the Secretary of State had been exposed to plague, John gave the number, emphasizing again only that it was a matter of utmost importance.

"Yes, yes," said the voice, sounding as if it was constantly besieged by such calls. "I'll take care of it."

Well, if I don't hear from him by morning, thought John, I'll let Oliver try. He might carry more weight.

No sooner had John hung up than the phone rang and he was informed by the hospital operator that Oliver wanted to see him in his office.

He found the administrator walking back and forth in front of his desk, his pudgy body bouncing with every stride. Oliver rubbed his fleshy hands together in an expression of satisfaction. His entire demeanor had changed and he now appeared to be exuberant.

"Well, John, those bastards are going to learn who they're messing with. Let them try to kick me out of their fucking country club—I'll take them to court on that, too. I just spoke to the U.S. attorney and he's going to call that greaser mayor of ours and if necessary, he'll get an injunction. The next thing you know there'll be federal marshalls in here." He laughed gleefully. "Try to mess with the Indian Health Service, will they. And if they think BIA will knuckle under to them, they're in for a surprise."

"I wish I could share your optimism," said John. "Tom Whitman says that Oglethorpe is a man to be reckoned with."

"Well, so is Russell Oliver. Don't worry about Oglethorpe. I'll take care of him."

John was surprised by Oliver's resistance to Oglethorpe's pressure and his willingness to fight back. In his three years at the hospital, John could not recall any show of strength on Oliver's part, or even the desire to become really involved in hospital matters. 'Don't make waves' was a reasonable assessment of the administrator's credo—until that morning's confrontation with Oglethorpe and his companions.

Their conversation was interrupted by the sound of the telephone buzzer. The administrator's face paled as he listened.

"John, there's been a cardiac arrest on the medical ward."

The two of them dashed from the office, both thinking of Bill Moore. The cardiac arrest team had already arrived on the floor and was working in one of the rooms with Stuart Hollander. John and Oliver quickly gowned and entered the room. The patient was not Bill Moore but Andrea Eagle, her face covered with an oxygen mask and a defibrillator on her chest. Her body arched into a spasm and heaved into the air as each shock was applied.

Hollander caught sight of Oliver. "She went into shock," he said, "then developed ventricular fibrillation."

He listened to her chest with his stethoscope and called for an ampule of adrenalin with a cardiac needle. The long needle was then deftly inserted between the woman's ribs directly into the heart muscle and the adrenalin injected. Once again Hollander listened. He removed the mask from her face and peered into the depths of her eyes with his ophthalmoscope.

"She's gone," he said.

"Shit!" exclaimed Oliver. "How come the antibiotics didn't hit the damn thing? She wasn't brought in too long after the symptoms started."

"In some cases," replied Hollander, "people die of plague despite antibiotic sterilization of their blood and tissues. There's probably a toxic effect directly on the heart and blood vessels."

"Five staff members with plague," groaned Oliver, "and three of them already dead. That's a hell of a batting average. It's going to scare the shit out of everyone in the hospital."

"Well, sir," said Hollander, interpreting the administrator's remarks as criticism of his treatment, "we're dealing with a very serious disease."

Russell Oliver glared over his mask at the young internist. "Who the hell said we weren't. What do you take me for, an idiot?"

"No sir, I just meant—"

Oliver swung on his heels and stormed out of the room, leaving the stammering Stuart Hollander standing helplessly at the bedside of the latest victim of the disease. The cardiac arrest team in the meantime slowly cleared away their equipment, their disappointment at their failure evident in their movements. They had ignored the altercation between Hollander and the administrator, their thoughts still focused entirely on the dead Indian nurse whom they had struggled in vain to save.

John accompanied Oliver back to his office. "Sometimes I wonder about that idiot, Hollander," fumed the administrator.

"He's a very competent internist," said John, willing to overlook his colleague's abrasive personality.

"Well, John, we've got a fine mess on our hands. More fuel for Oglethorpe's fire." The administrator's earlier confidence now seemed to be ebbing away.

"The important thing though," said John, trying to be reassuring, "is the appearance of new cases. We know we're going to lose some of the affected patients but if we can control the spread of the organism, we'll be all right. Where we seem to be luckiest is on the reservation with only three cases and all limited to the same family.

"Oh, one other thing," said John, suddenly remembering. "We neglected to call Sam Spencer and let him know about this. After all, he was the first one to have contact with the boy, Joseph Williams."

"Yes, and I wish now he had minded his own business," grumbled Oliver.

"I placed a call a little while ago to the State Department but they refused to put me through to him and I didn't want to go into details with anyone else. I spoke to some undersecretary named Dodson who said he'd give Spencer the message to call me."

"Hah!" exclaimed Oliver, lapsing into a fit of diabolical laughter. "That's what we really need. To give the fucking disease to the Secretary of State. I can see it now on the front page of the New York Times—Gallup Indian Hospital infects Secretary of State with plague—"

"It's not likely," smiled John, watching Oliver sink moodily into his desk chair. "He's preparing for the peace talks and he's obviously well or we would have heard something on the news. I don't think we have to worry but just to be on the safe side, I thought he should know."

"Oh, I agree with you, of course..."

"If he doesn't call back by tomorrow, I thought you could place the call to see if—"

"Sure, John," said Oliver, his flagging spirits momentarily revived as a result of this recognition of his position. "I'll take care of it. I think Sam Spencer will talk to me. He—"

A knock on the door interrupted him and a short, dark-haired man wearing glasses peered in.

"Come in, Ralph," called Oliver.

"Hi, Russ. Hi, John."

Ralph Germain had always reminded John of an owl. The tops of his ears were somewhat pointed and his thick spectacles, through which he always squinted, reinforced the impression. He was considered a first-rate pathologist and had worked at NIH and Walter Reed before joining the Indian Health Service. John recognized that he was methodical and conservative, never in a hurry to commit himself, but once he made a definitive pathologic diagnosis, there was no refuting it.

"I've been looking at the slides from Emma Hastings' lung sections," he announced, directing his remarks mainly to John. "She had a necrotizing pneumonia with extensive alveolar edema. We did smears on the fluid and found gram negative bacilli."

"Sounds confirmatory for plague," said John.

"Now, John," admonished the pathologist, "I'd agree that it sounds like a characteristic picture but other bacterial pneumonias have a similar appearance, you know. Before I commit myself I want to see the culture results."

"But we have bacteriologic confirmation already for the Williams boy."

"Yes, John, but the boy didn't come to postmortem and I'm a pathologist. I'd say, of course, that we have to proceed as if it were plague in view of the findings we've seen so far."

"You know you have two more posts to do,"said John.

"We're planning to do the one on Elsie Sims this afternoon. But I didn't hear about any other."

"Andrea Eagle, another nurse from Pediatrics, expired this morning."

"Oh! This is certainly becoming serious, isn't it?"

"That's the understatement of the century!" exclaimed Oliver. "Anyway, thanks, Ralph, for letting us know what you've found so far. Let me know your findings on the other two as soon as you have them. And we are proceeding as if it were plague—you've started your antibiotic, haven't you?"

"Well, as a matter of fact—"

"Down to the pharmacy—now!" said Oliver with irritation.

"I'm going," said the pathologist, making a hasty exit. John, feeling the rumblings of hunger and realizing it was past noon, left the office with him and headed for the cafeteria.

After having his plate filled with franks, beans and coleslaw, the special of the day, John sat down with some of the other physicians. No sooner had he touched the food with his fork, than he heard his name paged.

The doctor next to him laughed. "Good timing," he said. "You might have liked it if you had a chance to taste it."

"As usual," grumbled John. He took the call on the wall phone in the dining room and anyone watching would have seen him blanch perceptibly. He hastened back to the table and asked two of the other doctors, one a pediatrician and one a family practitioner, to accompany him to the Pediatrics ward.

"What is it, John?" asked one. "You look terrible."

"I'm going to need some help. The nurse on Peds thinks three of the kids on the ward have symptoms of plague."

"Jesus!" exclaimed the other pediatrician, letting his spoon fall from his hand.

"I was afraid of this because of the two cases we had in nurses who had worked on the ward, but I kept hoping it wouldn't happen."

The two physicians from whom John had requested assistance left their lunches and accompanied him to the ward. "No need to tell you, John," said one, "that many of the people in the hospital are getting scared. Since the meeting last night, the only talk we hear is about plague. I wouldn't be surprised if we start to see a lot of absenteeism among staff. It could hurt us on the wards."

"Especially with the news that three of the staff have died from the infection," emphasized the other. "It looks bad, John."

To John Hartman it looked even worse when he reached the ward. The three children, two boys of eight and six who were hospitalized for severe otitis media, and a girl of three with acute infectious diarrhea, were now all presenting with the same symptoms—high fever, headache and a rapid pulse rate. Each of them was acutely ill, flushed and restless, tossing and moaning in their beds.

"It started in the past hour with each of them," said the worried nurse."At first I thought it might just be a flareup of their original infections —but then I realized they were all too sick for that."

"We'll have to assume it's plague," said John, "and isolate them up on medicine. We can start Streptomycin therapy as soon as their bloods have been drawn."

Each of the three doctors examined one of the children and orders for their laboratory work and transfer were written. Within a half hour the children had been placed in the same isolation room on the medical ward and intramuscular Streptomycin was begun. The same stringent respiratory quarantine was put into effect for their room.

John had no thought now of returning to the cafeteria. The hunger he had felt earlier had been replaced by a knot of apprehension. How many more cases could he expect and how could he, in good conscience, admit any more patients to the Pediatrics ward now that the plague bacillus had made its appearance there? These were the questions that nagged at him as he headed back to the administrator's office.

This time Russell Oliver was not alone. Two men, each dressed in a business suit and carrying a briefcase, were in the office when John entered.

"Excuse me, sir," he said, "I must speak to you. It's urgent."

"Oh, come in, John. This is Mr. Herzog and Mr. Raymond from the Bureau of Indian Affairs in Washington. Gentlemen, this is Dr. Hartman, our chief of pediatrics. Dr. Hartman has been involved with this from the very beginning."

The men shook hands and Oliver looked questioningly at John. John hesitated and was about to ask again if he could see the administrator in private when Oliver indicated he could impart his message with the men being present. "Mr. Herzog and Mr. Raymond will be working closely with us on this, John."

"Well, I have more bad news. We've got three new cases, all among children on the Pediatrics ward. We've already transferred them to isolation on the Medical ward."

The two visitors from Washinton looked at one another and Oliver flushed and lowered his head. "The goddamn thing is beating us," he complained wearily.

"Well, Mr. Oliver," said Mr. Herzog, "this only reinforces what we were discussing. It's obvious that we're left with no choice."

"But, gentlemen," protested Oliver, "that does seem unreasonable—we've been putting our plague patients in isolation and managing to provide care to all our other patients. These three children are the first cases we've had among patients already in the hospital."

"Yes, Mr. Oliver," said Mr. Raymond in a heavy Georgian drawl, "it may be true that these are the first patients to become infected— but you have had five staff members with the disease and each of them, I'm sure, was in contact with patients. I expect you'll be seeing additional cases—it's just a question of time."

"It'll be a great hardship for the Navajos and for Shiprock," argued Oliver. "They're just not equipped to provide the range of services we do. Plague isn't the only problem for the Indians, as you well know."

Herzog gave a sigh of exasperation and turned to John. "You walked in in the middle of this, doctor, but what we've recommended is that the hospital admit only plague patients for the duration of the epidemic. All other cases will have to go to Shiprock. How do you feel about that?"

John hesitated, looking at each of them in turn and then at Oliver. "I think," he said finally, "that we really have no choice. I'd be very reluctant to admit any patients to Pediatrics at this point."

"John!" exclaimed the administrator, stunned at this reversal of opinion by his chief of pediatrics and unable to contain himself.

"It's for the best," said John slowly, hoping that Oliver wouldn't draw him into an altercation in front of the two visitors. "I just don't think we're justified in putting additional patients at risk. We can continue treating those patients we have in the hospital since we don't know whether or not they've already been exposed—but we can't take the chance of transmitting the infection to new admissions. I know it means converting the hospital into a communicable disease unit but what else can we do?"

Oliver shook his head. He knew that any further argument was now useless.

"Well, then," drawled Raymond, visibly pleased that John had supported him, "can we say that effective immediately there will be no further admissions to this hospital—except for patients with suspected plague?"

"I'll issue a directive," agreed a resigned Oliver.

"Also," continued Raymond, "we received a request from certain town officials that plague vaccine be administered by IHS. We feel that's inappropriate and unnecessary and will so inform them."

"What will happen to any Anglo in town who contracts the disease?" asked John.

The two visitors glanced quickly at one another. John caught the look and feared that Stanhope had been able to exert enough pressure on the Bureau for Calvary to avoid its responsibility for treating patients with plague.

Herzog chose to reply to the question and his answer only confirmed John's suspicions. "They'll have to be admitted to the hospital, of course."

'Which hospital?" persisted John.

"Well," replied Raymond, clearing his throat, "there have been suggestions made that such patients be admitted to this facility since it's the only one with known cases. Some people feel it would be unwise to expose another hospital to the disease. However, we've received no authorization to permit this facility to admit patients who are not Native American—staff excluded, of course."

John received the reply with surprise and wondered if the directness of his questions had made the two men vacillate. In any event, for the time being at least the hospital would remain a treatment center for the Indians. While John mulled this over in his mind, the BIA officials advised Oliver that they would remain in town for several days and meet with him regularly. He could, they assured him, expect their full cooperation. As soon as they had taken their leave, Oliver brought both hands down on his desk resoundingly.

"Jesus Christ, John! What the hell was the meaning—"

"We really had no choice," interrupted John. "How can we jeopardize every Indian that comes into this hospital? The three kids who've contracted the disease were in here for ear infections and diarrhea. How can we bring people in with diarrhea and put them at risk of getting pneumonic plague? It doesn't make sense."

Before Oliver could reply, John maintained the initiative. "Also, there was no mention of laying off staff or isolating hospital personnel or, for that matter, of denying access to Gallup for the reservation Indians. And they still hadn't acceded to Stanhope's request that we provide Anglos with services. So it appears that even though Oglethorpe and company put pressure on BIA, their demands were basically rejected. BIA must have been aware that caving in would raise a big stink. The Navajo Tribal Council would never have accepted those demands and there would have been lots of trouble. The Indians still won't like the cessation of admissions but I believe they can be made to see that it's in their best interest.

"In effect, the only proposal made by the mayor that was accepted by BIA was the one that was reasonable. I admit I didn't agree with it at first but after seeing those three children I had to concur."

"Well, John," grumbled Oliver, "maybe you're right—but I hate for that bastard, Oglethorpe, to think he's getting away with something."

"Oh, I don't think you have to worry about that—I suspect Mr. Oglethorpe is not going to be entirely happy about what's been decided—and not decided."

The events that occurred that same afternoon in Gallup bore out John's contention. A special noon edition of the local newspaper hit the streets with bold headlines announcing that plague had come to Gallup. The editorial page placed the blame for the outbreak on the "lax" policies of the IHS hospital and listed the mayor's recommendations, which, they made certain to note, had, with one exception, been unfavorably received by the IHS hospital administration. Within one hour after the paper's appearance, two Navajos employed at a local supermarket were set upon by a group of Anglo youths during their lunch break. The fight escalated as other Navajos and Anglos joined in. By the time the Gallup police appeared on the scene one Indian, a boy of seventeen, had been clubbed into unconsciousness and an Anglo man had a knife wound of the abdomen.

This initial spark ignited additional problems in the town. Groups of Navajos and Anglos fought at the local high school and classes were suspended for the remainder of the afternoon and for the following day. Storekeepers and saloon owners refused to sell to Indians, causing scattered clashes throughout the downtown area. Ultimately it appeared that Gallup was heading for its own version of vigilanteeism as small groups of Anglos parked their cars at strategic points to form roadblocks and prevent Navajos from leaving the reservation to enter Gallup. Local police and sheriffs were posted at these sites but seemed reluctant to precipitate trouble with their fellow townspeople. After much pleading and bargaining, they agreed to assist the men in "encouraging" Indians to return to the reservation provided that no violence was used. Fortunately, the presence of the uniformed men served as a deterrent and the majority of Indians returned peacefully to the reservation. Those that protested were either threatened or warned that their safety in Gallup could not be guaranteed.

John listened to these reports on an afternoon news broadcast in the doctor's lounge. The forebodings he had expressed earlier to Oliver werre proving warranted and he had no doubts about who was behind the violence now occurring in Gallup. Tom Whitman had also been correct in his assessment of the situation. Oglethorpe had resorted to the use of the press and as far as John knew, the reporters had still not even interviewed Oliver to hear what the hospital's viewpoint was. It would not have surprised John to learn that the editor of the Gallup newspaper was married to Oglethorpe's sister—which, in fact, he was.

He wondered how Oliver would react upon receiving the news and how far he would be willing to go in his struggle against Oglethorpe. Despite the assurances of the U.S. attorney there was now a de facto isolation of the reservation. John was certain that not every Navajo would be intimidated. The sporadic violence that had already occurred gave the promise of more problems to come. What particularly troubled John was the Anglo misreading of the situation. If they believed they could still exert absolute dominion over the Indians, they had been closing their ears to the increasingly militant pronouncements of both the Navajo and Hopi tribal councils. It was not inconceivable that full-scale fighting could break out and that, of course, would bring in the federal marshalls and probably the National Guard as well. But there would be blood shed before they could control the situation and the tensions would remain long after they were gone. John knew there were many Anglos in Gallup and on the surrounding ranches who would like nothing better than a chance to shoot a few Indians. And the young bucks on the reservation, those who were most vociferous in their demands for justice for Native Americans, would not hesitate to reciprocate carnage with carnage.

These thoughts weighed heavily on John as he left the hospital that evening for Beth's house. The atmosphere in Gallup remained tense and small groups of Anglo men milled around the downtown area. The normal crowd of Indians was conspicuously absent and the bars appeared to be virtually empty. He had not spoken to Russell Oliver again that afternoon and assumed that he was too involved in the pressing administrative affairs of the hospital and the rapidly deteriorating situation in Gallup. The directive had already gone out to all departments that only suspected plague cases were to be admitted. Other patients requiring hospitalization were to be transferred to Shiprock. Since no stipulation had been made about outpatient care, the administrator had decided to continue operation of all clinics. With the reservation effectively isolated, however, this was academic. In any event, John was certain that this, too, would cease as soon as it was brought to the BIA officials' attention.

CHAPTER 8 _____

THE SKY HAD ASSUMED A FIERY RED GLOW AS THE
day drew to an end. John drove slowly toward Beth's house, his
mind numbed by the events of the day and by the weariness that now
suffused his entire body. He almost regretted having made the
dinner date with Beth for he knew that if he could go directly home,
he would be asleep in a matter of minutes, and an escape into sleep
was what he craved most at the moment.

Beth lived in a small stucco house which she had been sharing
with her sister. They rented it from an uncle who had moved to Los
Angeles, she explained to John when he arrived, and now that Beth's
sister was to be married the following day, she would have the house
to herself.

Her individual touches were discernible everywhere. In each
room there were plants and flowers, and the windows were adorned
with bamboo shades. The walls were dominated either by shelves
lined with books or by exemplary Navajo rugs and paintings executed
by young Navajo and Mexican artists. Although it had the expected
boxlike construction, it was a house very different from any John had
ever visited in Gallup.

"I'll miss her," she said, speaking of her sister. "She's a few
years younger than I and I've always felt responsible for her since our
folks died. She's staying with her future in-laws in Winslow for a
couple of days, until the wedding tomorrow. Her husband—I guess I
should say husband-to-be—owns a furniture store there. It doesn't
sound very exciting but he's nice, Elena loves him, and it can't be
any worse than living in Gallup."

"Why do you stay in Gallup?" he asked.

She shrugged her shoulders. "When my mother died—that was only a year after my father was killed in a car accident—I was eighteen, terribly dependent, and very worried about my little sister who was only fourteen at the time. I met a man who worked here in town at an insurance ofice—he was quite a bit older, almost forty, but he wanted to marry me and since I was looking for a father figure that I could lean on, I accepted. I knew then that I didn't love him but I thought, or rationalized, that that would come in time. And at least I would have some security for my sister and for myself. To make a long story short, it didn't work out. I began working and as I became more independent, I realized what an unhappy situation I had put myself into. We parted—quite amicably—and he moved to Colorado where I understand he's doing very well. We still exchange Christmas cards." She smiled at the thought. "Since I was working when he left, I simply continued, and when my uncle left Gallup we had this house. I really can't complain—although Gallup can be very tedious."

"That still doesn't answer my question," he persisted, "and with your sister moving to Winslow, it would seem there's even less reason for you to stay."

Beth rested her chin on her finger and became thoughtful. John sat opposite her in a large stuffed chair in the living room sipping the wine she had poured for him. Except for the classical guitar music issuing softly from the record player, the room was now quiet.

"Perhaps I should mind my own business," he said at last, interpreting her silence as disapproval.

"No, it's a good question and one I've asked myself many times. I don't consider myself a provincial person but there are so many memories attached to this town—good memories. I was happy here as a child. I grew up in a house that was always filled with laughter. That's what made it so very difficult when my parents were gone. Everything changed and yet—" Her lips moved for a moment without speaking as she tried to formulate her thoughts. "And yet so much was unchanged. There was still the desert and the sky filled with stars and the sound of the train whistles at night. And all around me were my people. It was comforting and provided a solace that I needed."

She laughed suddenly and a flush, visible even in the soft light of the room, came to her cheeks. "I also like my job at the hospital if you'd prefer more mundane reasons."

John smiled in return. Gradually his body relaxed, succumbing to the wine and the comfort of the room, and above all to the presence of Beth, all creating a warmth and languor he had not experienced for longer than he could remember.

"You're quite a romantic, Beth Rodriguez. I think I'd prefer to accept the less mundane reasons."

"Who's the romantic?" she laughed. "I'd better take a look at our dinner—it should be almost ready."

As Beth disappeared into the kitchen, John let his head sink back on the chair. The wine combined now with his fatigue to make his eyelids heavy and several times he caught himself nodding into sleep. He struggled to stay awake, trying to concentrate on the sounds of Beth's movements in the kitchen, but to no avail. Suddenly, he awoke with a start to find Beth standing in front of him, the tenderest of smiles on her face.

"I imagine you've had a rough day," she said. "Would you like to take a nap before dinner?"

"I'm sorry," he apologized. "I know I'm not very stimulating company."

"No, I mean it—I wasn't being critical. You can lie down for a while and I'll reheat everything when you're ready to eat. There's one thing you should know right from the beginning—I don't stand on formality and if I make a suggestion, it's meant exactly the way it's said."

His hand automatically reached out to touch hers. "Thanks, Beth—but if I took a nap now I'm afraid I wouldn't wake up until breakfast. It's been that kind of a day."

"Well, then, how would you like some carne asada and salsa picante to wake you up right now?"

"That sounds wonderful. I knew I smelled something good."

They went into the kitchen, where Beth served by candlelight and refilled their wine glasses.

"This is very nice, Beth," he said, enjoying the fresh hot tortillas and tender slices of meat. "I'm sure glad we didn't go to one of the local greasy spoons."

She laughed. "Yes, Gallup is one of those towns where it's impossible to choose between restaurants—they're uniformly bad. They must figure that tourists passing through won't stick around long enough to complain and that the locals eat at home anyway."

Beth then brought the conversation around to the problems of the hospital and John, actually feeling relieved at the opportunity to discuss what had been happening, recounted for her the details of the plague outbreak from the very beginning.

She listened with rapt attention. When he had finished Beth gave an involuntary shudder. "It's quite frightening," she said.

"It is a terrible disease," he agreed. "But at least we have Streptomycin. In times past there was little that could be done."

"Yes, but Streptomycin didn't help Andrea Eagle," she countered. "Or the two other nurses. Andrea and I were close friends. In fact she was the dearest friend I had. I never knew a kinder, more generous person." Quickly she brushed her eyes. "I couldn't believe it when her husband called me today to tell me she had died."

They both watched the flickering candle and lapsed into a silence of their own thoughts. After a while John realized that she was weeping softly. "I'm sorry," she said. "I didn't want to spoil our evening and I've been trying hard to push it out of my mind. Crying at the dinner table is not standard procedure for me."

"I know how you must be feeling, Beth. These past few days have been a nightmare."

"Everyone at the hospital is frightened, you know."

"That's apparent. There's been a rash of psychosomatic complaints among staff—at the slightest sign of something amiss, any ache or pain, there's terror. Do you know that one of the nurses' aides on Peds asked me to examine her for plague this morning because she was hot and flushed? She was forty-nine, going through her menopause, and having these waves of heat and flushes for six months, but now they took on a new significance. And she didn't tell me that until after I had examined her."

Beth laughed and her eyes glistened through her tears. She's so lovely, John thought. He felt an overwhelming desire to reach out to her and take her in his arms.

"How long do you think it will go on, John?"

"It's impossible to say, Beth. I don't know which is worse right now—the actual outbreak or the secondary effects. Driving through town from the hospital this evening I felt as if I was in a tinder box that needed only one spark to set off a major fire. You can feel the tension."

An unwanted feeling of gloom settled over them. Sighing, Beth stood up and began to clear the table. John silently helped her and when the dishes were stacked, he touched her arm. "It was a delicious dinner, Beth. And I'll do the dishes."

"Thank you, kind sir, but such gallantry will not be necessary. You can dry though and keep me company."

Standing at the sink, he noticed the graceful curve of her neck and the thick black hair now removed from its pony tail and cascading over her shoulders. He thought that he could actually smell the nutmeg fragrance of her skin and he yearned to kiss her.

"I should never have brought up the subject of plague," she said. "It's not a good idea to carry hospital problems home. What I really wanted to talk about was you."

"Me? That's a very dull subject."

"Don't be modest. I've told you something about me."

"Well," said John, "I was born and raised in Boston and had a relatively uneventful and happy childhood. No brothers or sisters to have sibling rivalry with. My parents were very much in love with one another—still are, in fact—and always made me feel a part of that love. I somehow always knew I'd be a doctor although for a while I had dreams of being an artist."

"What finally decided you on medicine?"

"More than anything I think it was the influence of my Uncle Robert. He practiced general medicine for more than forty years in a small town on Cape Cod. We used to visit him several times a year and since Uncle Robert had no children of his own, I was his favorite—and only—nephew. He had a special interest in the history of medicine and during our walks on the beach he would tell me about Pasteur and Koch, Lister and Semmelweiss, and he made it all seem more exciting than any adventure I could imagine. Then when he went off on house calls, he would take me along with him and introduce me as his assistant. That was heady stuff for a ten year old. Years later I came to the conclusion that Uncle Robert had really been very clever in steering me toward a career in medicine and that he always hoped I'd follow in his footsteps." He smiled at the recall of a sudden memory. "I went to Yale for my undergraduate work and then medical school in Boston. On the day I graduated from med school, Uncle Robert was there with my folks. He congratulated me and gave me a beautiful leather doctor's bag with my name on it in gold letters. 'Do you know when I had your name put on that?' he asked me. 'When you were about eleven or twelve years old'."

Beth laughed. "I guess you were right about Uncle Robert."

"Well, anyway, I met my wife while I was in school. She was a commercial artist. We were married during my internship and then moved to San Diego for my pediatrics residency. Janet hated San Diego, couldn't find the work she wanted, and lived for the day she could go back east."

John lapsed into silence and there was an uncomfortable pause.

"I know you're divorced," said Beth. "Do you miss her?"

"No." He sighed deeply, then told her about Valentina.

"Oh, John, how terrible for you. It's such a tragic story."

"It's taken me a long time to get over it. I don't know if I ever really will. And so, I was at loose ends and ended up joining the Indian Health Service. I've been in Gallup three years now. I enjoy my work, feel I've learned a great deal professionally and from the Indians, and where else can you get such wonderful desert sunrises and sunsets?"

"You really do have a romantic streak then. I always thought from seeing you in the hospital that you were so scientific, so very serious."

"It's all an act," he laughed. "Underneath it all there's the soul of a Gaugin, yearning to express itself."

"Well," she said, putting the last of the dishes in the cupboard, "let's sit in the living room, have some more wine, listen to music, and you can tell me about your yearning soul."

Beth turned off the lights and placed the dinner candles on a coffee table. She poured more wine for them and they sat on the sofa watching the dancing patterns of the candlelight and listening to the music of Tarrega and Granados played by Segovia. They turned to look at one another and impulsively John leaned over and kissed her lips. They were soft and yielding and tasted of wine.

"Your yearning soul is beginning to express itself," she smiled.

"Now you're teasing me."

"I wouldn't do that," she said, placing her glass on the table and taking his face between her hands. She again brought his lips to hers in a long, velvety kiss that had the blood in his temples throbbing. He groped for the table to put his glass down and then drew her closer to him. The firm curves of her breasts pressed against his chest and he pressed his lips to the curve between her neck and shoulder.

Without saying anything, she extracted herself from his embrace, stood up and extended her hand. He clasped it in his and she led him into her bedroom where she began to undress. He removed his own clothes, watching Beth's glowing silhouette in the moonlight that filtered through the window. Her body was slender, yet voluptuous, and his senses reeled as she drew him toward her on the bed. He buried his face between her breasts and inhaled the spicy fragrance of her skin while his hands explored her body, touching the soft mounds and inviting recesses of each curve, and then suddenly he was inside of her.

His excitement was intense and his body threatened an immediate release, but Beth's voice murmured in his ear, soothing and calming him, while her fingers moved across his skin, stroking and fondling. Gradually his fear of coming prematurely subsided and he allowed himself to be led by the slow rhythmic movement of Beth's hips, his own hands cupping her firm breasts with their erect nipples and then sliding down to feel the moist softness between her thighs and the sensuous roundness of her buttocks.

He followed Beth willingly, letting her set the pace, and gradually her pelvis thrust harder and harder. As she whispered in his ear, "now, my love," he felt the floodgates of his passion open and his entire body wrench in a spasm of release that elicited a sharp cry which merged with Beth's luxurious groan of pleasure. His orgasm lasted longer than any he could remember and when, at last, it subsided and his body rested firmly against Beth's, the two now seemingly inseparable, he felt every care and frustration had been dissipated by the intensity of their lovemaking.

Enveloped in the cool silence of the New Mexico evening, neither one dared to shatter the mood to which they now happily abandoned themselves. It was only when a desert breeze came through the open window and stroked their bodies, causing them both to shiver simultaneously, that Beth said, "we'd better get under the covers."

He held her in his arms, inhaling the aroma of their lovemaking and feeling sensations of love and desire that had been absent for years.

"Beth," he murmured softly, "that was wonderful and I think I might be falling in love with you."

"I feel the same way, John."

The silence returned but he knew she was awake and thinking.

"John?"

"Yes?"

"Do you think you can ever forget the past?"

"There's an old saying," he replied, "that beginnings are always difficult. I think this is an exception."

"I like that," she said. "New beginnings."

Their bodies still entwined, they fell into a deep sleep in which John found himself dreaming and restless. He was being subjected to terrible tortures by unseen demons who had turned his head into an anvil upon which their hammers beat incessantly while a fiery inferno threated to consume him. At last he moaned loudly, no longer able to bear the agonizing discomfort, and the sound of his cry woke him. Beth also came awake with a start and gasped.

"John, your body is burning up. Do you have a fever?"

The intensity of the pain behind his temples provided him with the answer. "I think Bill Moore is going to have company," he said weakly.

CHAPTER 9 _____

UNDERSECRETARY ELWOOD DODSON HUNG UP THE
phone with a soft oath. Why the hell would a doctor in Gallup, New
Mexico want to talk to the Secretary of State? he wondered. He was
past the point, of course, where any call was an occasion of surprise.
The phone had rung continuously that entire day with people all over
the world wanting to talk to Spencer. Some were well-wishers, others
had advice to give, and then there were the kooks—the leftists and
rightists of radical bent, the fanatics who threatened that the wrath of
God was imminent, and an assorted collection of unhospitalized
psychotics. He wished that Spencer's secretaries would do a better
job of screening the calls.

Williams placed the message with John Hartman's name and
phone number in a memo envelope to Spencer and dropped it in his
outgoing box. He knew it was destined to become part of a
mountainous pile of similar messages on the Secretary's desk, most
of which would never be answered. Mail and calls to State were
always heavy. But in times of crisis or when major events like the
present peace conference occurred, there was a deluge that required
additional temporary help as well as overtime from regular workers.

Elwood Dodson on this day had been relegated to the office to
manage the unusually large number of employees present on a
Saturday and to oversee the routine operations of the department.
He reflected bitterly on the fact that after a twenty-seven year career
in the diplomatic service and State Department he was being put in
the position of office manager while preparations for the most
important peace conference in decades were taking place. If
anything, he felt his place was at Spencer's side. In actuality, he

believed, and would admit this to no one but his wife, who, of course, shared the same view, his place was in Spencer's shoes.

When the President had announced Spencer's appointment as Secretary, Elwood Dodson had felt betrayed. "I have given twenty-five years to my country," he said to his wife on that day of sorrow as he downed his fourth martini, "and this is how I'm repaid."

Williams was Undersecretary at the time of Spencer's appointment and was certain that even that position would be taken away from him. Unbeknownst to him, however, the President had advised Sam Spencer to retain the Undersecretary. "He's an asshole but a perfect functionary for all the hackwork and bullshit your office will get. You'll have your hands freed for the more important matters. If you were to get rid of him," reasoned the President, "and Lord knows I thought your predecessor would many times since Dodson is a pompous little prig and difficult to take on an empty stomach, you'd have to train someone else while you were getting your own feet wet."

When Spencer accepted the President's advice and personally asked Dodson to stay on, the Undersecretary had graciously replied, "I'm honored, Mr. Secretary," while thinking that 'the son of a bitch realizes he can't get along without me'.

And now, a few years later, on this lovely June morning in Washington, his dedication had gotten him totally excluded from preparations for the biggest Mideast peace conference in history. With the overthrow of the mullahs in Iran and Saddam in Iraq, those two countries would participate in what promised to be an epochal development for the region. To make matters worse, he and his wife had received an invitation a week earlier from Henry Carstairs, president of General Motors, to join him on this very Saturday for a sail on his yacht off the Maryland shore. He had known already that he would be required to remain in the office the entire day but seeing the disappointed expression on his wife's face as he declined the invitation, he had suggested that she go in his stead. Although she tactfully demurred, Carstairs had insisted, as she must have known he would, and at this very moment they were probably sailing under a clear blue sky, relaxing with their martinis on the deck of Carstairs's magnificent yacht, a photograph of which he had once seen in the Washington Post.

He pictured Patricia in her swimsuit, drink in hand, laughing that girlish giggle of hers which had so charmed him twenty years earlier. He knew now that the laugh, as well as everything else about Patricia, was studied. Her New Orleans socialite mother had instructed her in all the accepted mannerisms of southern womanhood and Patricia had been a good pupil. Even now, in her midforties, she was a handsome woman. She took almost a narcissistic pride in her small, slender body, and not only had she not gained a pound since their marriage in spite of having had two children, but she exercised religiously and wore fashions that few women her age would dare. Williams frowned when he thought of Carstairs—he was a good man to know, of course, but he did have a reputation as a rake, which his being close to sixty had not helped to diminish. It was true that he was bald and had an ample paunch, but twenty million dollars tended to blind people to unpleasant physical attributes. He had neglected to ask Carstairs if other people would be accompanying them and now he cursed himself for his oversight and for his stupidity in urging Patricia to go.

Tapping nervously on the desk, he picked up a sheaf of papers and tried to read the reports they contained. When he had read the same paragraph five times, he sighed and threw the papers down in disgust.

His fantasies were now totally out of control and he imagined Carstairs and Patricia lying nude on the deck of the boat, their bodies entwined. He found himself hating them for making a cuckold of him, hating Spencer for relegating him to the office, and hating his colleagues who had helped set up the conference in the first place.

"Hello!" he bellowed angrily into the phone as the buzzer rang, frightening the secretary who was calling to ask if she could take her lunch break.

"What? Yes, yes—you can go now." He hung up and then paced nervously around the office.

It was all preposterous, of course. He knew that he was not thinking rationally and he chided himself for it. Patricia had always been faithful to him. He was sure of that. But even as he reassured himself, an old memory returned to spur his doubts. There was the time in Liberia when he had been ambassador. They had had servants, of course, and one of them, a young black giant who even he had to admit was a handsome specimen, had apparently caught his wife's fancy. "He's so gentle," she said. "Harmless really. And he'll do anything I tell him."

Even though it had made him nervous to have the man around, he indulged his wife's whims, as he always had, and said nothing. Then one day he had returned unexpectedly to the house about noon to pick up some papers he had forgotten. Passing under the bedroom window, which was on the second floor of the house and opened onto a terrace, he distinctly heard Patricia's giggle coming through the open terrace doors.

Another servant, trimming hedges in front of the house, noticed what had occurred and said loudly, "Good day, Mr. Ambassador. Home early today, I see."

Dodson ignored the man and hurriedly entered the house, a disturbing suspicion nagging at his mind. He walked quickly up the stairs and entered the bedroom without knocking. His wife was lying in bed—alone—with a cloth across her eyes.

Dodson glanced quickly around the room. There was no one there but the doors to the veranda were now closed. Saying nothing, he opened them and stepped out on the balcony. It was only about ten feet above the ground, an easy drop for a tall man. He saw no sign of anyone but the servant trimming hedges, who looked up and noticed him. A gold tooth glistened as he smiled at the ambassador and bowed slightly.

"Why, Elwood," said his wife, suddenly sitting up in bed, "you're home early. I've had a terrible headache all morning."

He had mumbled something about her taking some aspirin, picked up his papers, and left. That same afternoon he had had his wife's "gentle" servant transferred and neither he nor Patricia every discussed it.

The memory had rankled for years but nothing else had occurred in Liberia or in future assignments to arouse any suspicions of infidelity. Gradually, not only had the memory receded, but Dodson, in those rare moments when he did think of Liberia, had come to dismiss his wife's suspected transgression as a figment of his own imagination.

And now, on a beautiful June day, due to his own maneuverings, he was once again assailed by the fears that had lain dormant for so long. Goddamn her, he thought. And Carstairs. And Spencer. His small fist thudded against the desk and he winced with the pain.

Glaring at the cloudless blue sky visible from his office window, he sighed, then opened the bottom left hand drawer of his desk and removed the bottle of Beefeater. He knew it was going to be a long day.

CHAPTER 10 _____

THE WEEK HAD STARTED BADLY FOR SAM SPENCER. His delayed return from Albuquerque had forced the cancellation of one policy meeting at the White House, adding to the President's annoyance at him for having gone to Flagstaff—and without Secret Service protection—only one week in advance of the peace talks.

To make matters worse, certain changes had come over him, subtly at first in the form of a strange lethargy that he attributed to jet lag, but with each passing day the alterations in his behavior became more pronounced. It was not unusual for Sam Spencer to work fifteen hour days. During times of crisis, he had often gone for two or three nights without sleep, stealing only an occasional catnap, and his faculties had remained unimpaired. Now, however, the intense concentration that he prided himself on had begun to slip. At the daily round of meetings with the President and his advisers, and with the Joint Chiefs and members of Congress, there were disturbing lapses, moments when his attention drifted away and he found himself immersed in images conjured from the past. Perhaps it was normal for these memories to be provoked by Julia's funeral but he felt himself suddenly vulnerable, open to feelings of loneliness that he had never before experienced. Who will mourn me when I die? he thought morosely. He envisioned another stone next to the graves of Kate and Jeff, one that had his name inscribed with the epitaph "unloved and unremembered".

And perhaps, too, it was normal that once a breach had been made in the defenses he had so assiduously erected over the years, he should begin to question the very doctrines that governed his life and his work. Sam Spencer did not consider himself either a Machiavellian or a politician but rather a pragmatist, totally dedicated to his country and to the protection of its interests. The solutions to some problems, he knew, were going to be unpalatable to anyone with a strict moral sense—but morality was a luxury in international relations that no major power could afford.

The present upcoming peace talks were a case in point. During the bargaining sessions that would occur, each nation would press its demands, securing what it could for itself while giving up as little as possible. And if the final agreements, assuming the successful resolution of most of the issues, involved major changes that would directly affect the future of people such as the Kurds or the sovereignty of countries such as the emirates, that was a price that had to be paid in the name of international peace.

"Horse trading among thieves" was what his father would have called it, but Amos Spencer had been a Congressman in times that were less complex, during those halcyon days when international terrorism and mushroom clouds did not threaten the world. It was easier then to be selfrighteous and bandy about words like "honesty" and "morality".

Sam had never felt the need to justify his actions. Now, however, he suddenly found himself arguing his position in silent dialogues with his long dead father. Somehow the words rang hollow and he considered himself put in the position of a man attempting to defend the indefensible. And then he wondered what Kate would say if she could listen to the arguments. Would she even recognize him as the same man she had loved and married—never truly liberal or visionary, but dedicated and decent in his own conservative way? Would she have been impressed by his explanations of the validity of using certain illegitimate means to attain certain essential ends? He found himself silently pleading for her understanding yet knowing that she, like his father, would have been unable to accept his views or condone his complicity in certain dealings of his government.

Julia, of course, would have reacted with horror to his defense of what in her mind was unethical and immoral—but Julia's world had been a circumscribed one, a world limited to white men and Indians in a remote corner of the United States. I am not an idealistic doctor like John Hartman or a lawyer attempting to redress the wrongs of society, argued Sam—I am a statesman, a combatant in an international arena.

It would have been impossible for any of them to understand

the pressures under which he labored, but for some inexplicable reason he felt it important now to convince these people whom he had loved, dead though they may be, that he, Sam Spencer, was an honorable man.

That Saturday morning he had awakened at five A.M. from only four hours of a restless sleep, the incessant ring of his alarm clock reverberating within his skull as he sat on the edge of the bed. Even after the clock had been silenced, the discomfort behind his temples persisted, only now it had taken on the character of a pulsating throb. Staggering into the bathroom, he stepped immediately into the shower, where he turned on only the cold water faucet. The icy needles assaulted his skin, evoking an involuntary gasp and precipitating him into a state of wakefulness. The headache, however, remained, firmly lodged now behind his eyes and was aggravated even by the motion of drying himself. The pain made it difficult for him to look at his reflection in the mirror as he shaved. It was a hell of a time, he thought, to have a headache like this, especially since he could count on the fingers of one hand the number of times in his life when he had been afflicted with one.

Sam took the aspirin bottle from the medicine chest and gulped two of the tablets. Within moments, his stomach reacted violently and he barely had time to get his head over the toilet. The force of his initial vomiting brought him to his knees, while his hands clutched the rim of the bowl. Once the tablets were expelled with the small amount of liquid he had taken, a succession of dry heaves left him gasping and struggling to regain his breath. When at last the feeling of nausea subsided, he managed to stand up, leaning on the sink for support.

He stared at his pale reflection in the mirror and noted a prominent blood spot adjacent to the pupil of his right eye, the result of a capillary's rupture during his siege of vomiting. The headache had increased in intensity and he winced with every movement of his head. "Christ, Spencer," he said aloud, "you're a mess. Of all the wrong days to have it happen." His driver would be picking him up at seven and he would have breakfast with the President at seven-thirty.

While he dressed, moving slowly so as not to exacerbate the pain in his head, he ruminated on the possible causes of his sudden indisposition. The previous evening's banquet at the White House with members of Congress and foreign dignitaries had been a sumptuous feast but Sam, as always, had eaten lightly and his drinking had been limited to two glasses of wine. It was almost inconceivable that he had food poisoning. Unable to come up with any explanation, he decided it was a virus, probably of the twenty-four hour variety.

He walked to the window and parted the drapes. The glare of daybreak pierced his senses with the shock of a swordthrust, making him wince with the intensified pain he felt in his head. Staggering backward, he sat down heavily on the sofa and closed his eyes. A sudden chill caused his entire body to tremble and he noticed, too, that he had developed an irritating dry cough. Beads of perspiration broke out on his forehead and he knew that he had a fever. Ordinarily a one or two degree rise in his temperature did not cause Sam too much discomfort. He placed the back of his hand against his temples and guessed by the heat being given off that he had at least 102. He thought of asking Dr. Peterson, the President's physician, to check him over, but decided that would have to wait until after the meeting.

The ring of his telephone startled him. Sam stood up with difficulty and walked unsteadily to the phone. It was his driver informing him that he would be there in five minutes. Sam hung up and went into the bathroom, where he washed his face repeatedly with cold water. He thought of trying the aspirin again but doubted that the pills would stay down.

The coughing had become even more troublesome than the headache and he rummaged through the medicine cabinet searching for an old bottle of cough syrup. The assorted jars, tubes, and bottles began to swim before his eyes and he clutched at the sink to steady himself. He closed his eyes tightly in an effort to control the sudden attack of vertigo but the entire room was now spinning violently and he felt the floor go out from under his feet. The last thing Sam noticed was the glare of the light bulb on the ceiling, a distant sun with its own corona that flickered for a moment before the darkness came.

CHAPTER 11 _____

THE STAFF AT WALTER REED HAD BEEN ALERTED TO the Secretary of State's arrival and Colonel Marcus Silver, chief of internal medicine, had personally taken charge of the case. The Colonel was a graduate of the University of Rochester School of Medicine and had gone on to attain fame for his work in hematology and infectious disease at Peter Bent Brigham. He had been in the Army for eighteen years and it was almost certain that a promotion to General was imminent.

He stood now at Sam Spencer's bedside with William Peterson, the White House physician, looking down at Sam's unconscious form as the Secretary was undressed by two nurses.

"You say that Mr. Spencer has shown no signs of being ill?" asked Dr. Silver, the skepticism in his voice unmistakable .

"Not as far as I know," replied Dr. Peterson in a Texas drawl. "The President was shocked when I informed him right after receiving the call from Mr. Spencer's driver this morning. Mr. Spencer appeared to be in good health when they met yesterday. Of course, with a position like his one never knows. I don't believe a person with Mr. Spencer's responsibilities would know he was ill until he was almost moribund. I can vouch for that having seen the President walk around with a high fever and bronchopneumonia for days at a Joint Chiefs' meeting. And that's strictly confidential," he cautioned. "The press never got hold of that one."

Dr. Silver gave an understanding nod, then began his examination. After checking vital signs, he proceeded to evaluate Sam Spencer's organ systems. The nurses stood in attendance as he worked, handing him whatever diagnostic instrument he needed and moving the Secretary of State into the appropriate postion. Dr.

Peterson stood by silently, the only sign of his anxiety an occasional glance at his wristwatch. He knew that the President was awaiting his call and that the White House policy meeting was soon to begin.

"Well," said Dr. Silver, concluding with a testing of reflexes, "it's an unusual case. Temperature 104.8, pulse 142, BP normal, and obvious cyanosis. I hear some rhonchi and wheezing but his lungs are resonant and there are no rales. There's little else to provide a clue. And look here." He pointed to several areas on Sam Spencer's thorax and thighs that were covered with small discolored patches. "They look like ecchymoses. It's perplexing. I've seen fulminating influenzal syndromes but I don't believe that's what we're dealing with." He looked at one of the nurses, a grey-haired officious woman, and began to give his orders. "Let's get a stat CBC, urinalysis with culture and sensitivity, general health screen, bleeding profile, blood culture, EKG and chest X-Ray for starters. Keep him in isolation with no visitors. I'll also want vital signs every 15 minutes and you can start an IV with a liter of Ringer's lactate, 100 cc per hour. I want him on intake and output so put a Foley in. Let's set up for a lumbar puncture. I'll send up MacPherson for that. If there's any change in his condition I want to be called immediately. I'll be back after the lab work, LP and chest X-Ray are done and give orders for antibiotic coverage."

'Yes, doctor," she replied, nodding to the other nurse to remain as she left the room to initiate the orders.

Dr. Silver looked thoughtfully at Sam and then turned to the other nurse, a young blond woman of no more than twenty-two who appeared awed at the responsibility of caring for the Secretary of State. "Miss Andrews, please tell the technicians that I want to be called as soon as the lab work, tracing and X-Ray results are available."

"Yes, sir," she replied, a quaver in her voice betraying her anxiety.

"It's all so sudden," said Peterson as they left the room. "Unbelievable really. It couldn't have happened at a worse time."

"There never is a good time for an illness—especially for someone in Mr. Spencer's position. Would you like some coffee, Dr. Peterson, while we wait for lab results?"

"Yes, thank you."

The two men headed for the cafeteria while back in the room

they had just left, Sam Spencer hovered on the brink of consciousness but was unable to take the final step across. He mumbled incoherently in his delirium and tossed restlessly in the bed as the nurse inserted a needle in his forearm for administration of intravenous fluids.

Dr. Silver sat with Dr. Peterson in the hospital cafeteria, the two men thoughtfully sipping their coffee. "It's odd," mused the Colonel. "Whatever he has apparently came on with an explosive onset. And whatever the causative organism is it appears to be having an endotoxic effect on blood vessels. That would be my guess, at least after seeing those ecchymoses. I hope we can grow something out on the cultures and get him stabilized until then."

"What will you start him on while you wait for culture results?"

"If the WBC and diff indicate a bacteriological pathogen, which I think they will, I'd be inclined to start him on Gentamycin and Ancef, but I'd better put in a call for Heaney and Castillo, our communicable disease experts, to see him in consultation. We'll see what they say."

"I hope you'll notify me if there's any change in his condition. The President wants to be kept closely informed. You can imagine his concern."

"I'll keep in touch with you on a regular basis, Dr. Peterson. Don't worry about that. You can reassure the President that he'll be kept closely advised as to Mr. Spencer's status."

The two men broke off their conversation as Dr. Silver's name was announced on the paging system. Excusing himself, he went to the wall phone where Peterson could see him nodding but could not hear what was being said.

"We've got some results back," said Silver, returning to the table. "WBC 13,250 with a slight shift to the left so we'll have to assume it's bacterial. I'd better give Heaney and Castillo a call and head over to X-Ray. Oh, by the way, did you bring his medical file with you?"

"No, but I'll have it sent over by messenger right away. Past history is really quite uneventful—he's always been in good health."

"No allergies to medications?"

"None that I'm aware of."

"Well, fine then, Dr. Peterson." The two men stood up and shook hands. "I'll get back to you this afternoon and let you know how he's doing."

The Colonel placed his call to the two infectious disease specialists and then stopped in the X-Ray Department to review Sam Spencer's films. The X-Rays revealed a diffuse pneumonitis involving both lungs, including the apices.

Strange, mused Silver, rhonchi and wheezes but no rales. The picture is worse than the clinical findings. He headed back up to Spencer's room and found him being attended by both nurses. They looked up anxiously as he entered. 'He appears to be worse, Dr. Silver," said the grey-haired nurse. "Very restless, pulse 160 and irregular. He's coughing a lot and brought up some blood-tinged mucus."

Colonel Silver looked down at the flushed, sweating face of Sam Spencer. A trickle of rust-colored sputum had appeared at the corners of his mouth and the doctor requested a culture tube. He then listened to his patient's heart and lungs and frowned.

"Put a call in for a cardiology consult. I think Dr. Benton is on today. Dr. Heaney and Dr. Castillo will be here shortly to see Mr. Spencer. Please call me when they get here."

By the following morning Sam Spencer had been seen by a team of specialists. He had been digitalized and had received almost twenty-four hours of intensive antibiotic therapy. His condition, however, remained unchanged, increasing Dr. Silver's concern. Not only was there no amelioration of the signs of toxicity, but he had still not regained consciousness. Because of his worsening cough and obvious shortness of breath, oxygen was being administered. Copious amounts of liquid sputum were now being produced and another sample had been sent for culture. At times he flailed about wildly, threatening to dislodge his intravenous catheter, and then suddenly all movement ceased and he would appear to lapse into a deep comatose state. To add to Dr. Silver's woes, the news of the Secretary's hospitalization had been leaked to the press and the hospital was now besieged by reporters. By early afternoon on that Sunday it was obvious that a statement would have to be given. Colonel Silver had already been on the phone once that day with the President. The second conversation was one he would not quickly forget.

"He's still not conscious?" asked the Commander-in-Chief.

"No, sir. He hasn't responded."

"This is incredible. Colonel, I must know your candid opinion of what we can expect."

"Mr. President, I wish I could be more sanguine but the Secretary's condition is extremely precarious at the moment. I'd have to say his prognosis is poor—unless some dramatic change occurs between now and tomorrow morning. He's had more than twenty-four hours of antibiotic therapy with no response. Until we get a culture report back that lets us know what organism we're dealing with, it's all guesswork."

"When will you have a culture report?"

"If there's going to be any growth, it should become apparent by the morning. Mr. President, it's going to be necessary for me to make a statement to the press. The reporters have been here all day. Would you like to make a recommendation as to what we should tell them?"

"Yes. Tell them that Mr. Spencer has left us with a fucking mess."

"Sir?"

"Goddammit, Colonel, do you have any idea of the situation we're in?"

"But, sir, the man is seriously ill—it's not—"

"I don't need your explanations, Colonel. I need my Secretary of State. These meetings are simply too important. I find it hard to believe that with all the experts at your disposal, you can't make a diagnosis and treat this thing."

"Sir, couldn"t you postpone—"

"No! The meetings will have to continue with or without him—it's too late to postpone them. Spencer was indispensable to us—and now—oh, Christ, what's the use? How could he do this to us?"

Colonel Silver listened incredulously, reluctant to reply.

"Listen, Colonel, tell those press idiots that the Secrtary has a bad case of the flu with a high temperature. Even though it doesn't look good for him right now, maybe we'll get a miracle and he'll recover enough in a day or two to participate in the talks."

"I would seriously doubt—"

"I don't give a shit what you seriously doubt! Just do as I tell you, Colonel. If things take a turn for the worse, we'll cross that bridge when we come to it. I want to hear from you again this evening." "Yes, sir, of—"

Before the words were out of Colonel Silver's mouth, the President had hung up. The Colonel had never been a man to give way under pressure. In Vietnam he had earned the Congressional Medal of Honor, an unheard of award for a doctor-officer but one merited for his valiant efforts to save the patients at TucDo hospital before it was overrun by the North Vietnamese. He had also managed to accrue a Silver Star and two Purple Hearts during his illustrious military career, making him the most decorated physician in the Army's history. At the moment, however, Dr. Marcus Silver slumped dejectedly in his chair and dabbed with his handkerchief at his perspiring brow. Being berated by a President was a new experience and made the hail of enemy rocket fire at TucDo seem a picnic in comparison.

CHAPTER 12 _____

RUSSELL OLIVER, ENSHROUDED IN A CAP AND GOWN, peered over his surgical mask at John Hartman and Bill Moore and shook his head. "This is a hell of a thing," he grumbled. "Two department heads flat on their asses in bed. Is that any way to run a hospital?"

"That's just what I was thinking," grimaced Bill, restlessly shifting his position in bed in a vain effort to get more comfortable. An intravenous solution dripped into the arms of both men and Bill's gaze shifted to the suspended bottle. His face was deeply flushed and the perspiration on his skin glistened in the room's dull light.

John Hartman, in the adjoining bed, groaned and opened his eyes.

"How do you feel, John?" asked Oliver.

"Awful."

"That seems to be the prevalent feeling around here. Well, if it's any consolation to you two, Hollander says you're holding your own and he expects that you'll be responding to the Streptomycin within the next twenty-four hours."

John motioned weakly to the water pitcher at his bedside and the administrator poured a glass for him, then helped support his head so he could drink it. He felt the heat emanating from John's body and noticed that the bedding was saturated with sweat.

"I'll have one of the girls change your bedding," he said solicitously.

"I think they did it about three times during the night," said Bill. "Five minutes later everything is soaked again. If only this fever would break..."

"At least we're right on top of it with you two. You'll be okay."

"What else is happening?" asked John, his voice a hoarse whisper.

"Well, one positive development. No new cases in the past twelve hours. At least none that we know of. We also received visitors from CDC in Colorado this morning and they recommended that everyone in the hospital be put on prophylactic Tetracycline."

"Probably not a bad idea," said Bill Moore. "I wish John and I had started taking it earlier."

"We have the families of those who've already contracted the disease on antibiotics. Can either of you think of someone you might have been in contact with after symptoms started?"

"Someone out of the hospital you mean?" asked Bill.

"Yes."

"Are all employees receiving Tetracycline?" asked John.

A smile flickered across Oliver's lips. "Yes—all. Which reminds me, John." He placed a small wrapped package he had been holding on the night table next to the bed. "A certain young lady asked me to deliver this to you. And in case you're wondering, she's also on antibiotics."

"Thank you," John replied, his voice barely audible.

Bill Moore turned to look at John and attempted to raise himself on his elbows. The effort proved to be too much. "Well, well," he murmured, sinking back onto his pillow.

Russell Oliver fidgeted nervously as he watched their suffering. Hollander had sounded optimistic, yet...He looked again from one to the other as each of them had seemingly drifted into a semi-sleep, oblivious now of his presence. The only sound in the room was that of each man's harsh, rapid breathing. Turning to leave, he suddenly heard John's voice.

"Is everything all right in town?"

"Yes, John. No more trouble. Don't worry about it. Just try to rest and lick this thing. Oh, by the way, I gave you one gift but forgot the other." Reaching into his pants pocket beneath the gown, he withdrew a small object and placed it in John's limp hand. "Some old Indian gave me this to give you. He said it would help in—what the hell were his words?—in—finding the way and walking in beauty."

John raised the object before his eyes and nodded. It was a rattle made of animal skin and covered with feathers.

"It must be from Sam Begay," he whispered.

Oliver snorted behind his mask. "I don't know what the hell to say, John. An Indian medicine man and a beautiful senorita sending you gifts and you lying here with the goddamn plague. It's unreal. I can't take my eyes off you for a minute."

John forced a smile. "You worry too much. Didn't you hear Hollander say we'd be fine. Besides—I have powerful medicine." He extended the rattle toward the administrator.

Oliver laughed in spite of himself. "You're nuts—that fever must be getting to you."

"Hey, John," called Bill Moore, his eyes still closed. "How about shaking that thing over me."

The administrator looked quickly from one to the other. "Jesus," he moaned, "they're both delirious."

As he left the hospital he breathed deeply. It was a beautiful summer afternoon with a cloudless sky, the kind of day that ordinarily would have found Russell Oliver on the golf course. But that was before the plague had entered their lives and turned the world topsy-turvy. He considered going out to the country club for a few quiet hours on the putting green but the thought of encountering Oglethorpe and his friends dissuaded him. "Bastards," he growled.

He sat down in his car and wondered how to pass the remaining hours of Sunday. There was still paper work to be done but he couldn't face the prospect of returning to his office. If he were to go home, his wife would find a million and one chores for him and he would be compelled to listen to her incessant chatter. He drummed impatiently on the steering wheel, uncertain of where to go. Looking at his watch he saw that it was about time for another dose of Tetracycline. He reached into the glove compartment and removed a bottle of capsules and a half-pint flask. "I won't forget to take these," he said softly, the memory of the fever-ravaged faces of John Hartman and Bill Moore still fresh in his mind. He washed the antibiotic down with a swallow of bourbon and licked his lips contentedly. That was always a possibility for a Sunday afternoon, he thought with a grin—a secluded spot outside of town where he could forget he had ever heard of the goddamn plague and concentrate on emptying the contents of his flask. There wasn't enough to really tie one on but it would provide good company while it lasted.

He turned the key in the ignition and drove north after leaving the hospital lot. There were several arroyos a short distance from town where he could find some shade and not have to be concerned with meeting anyone. Traffic became lighter once he was outside the environs of Gallup and he turned on the radio. The sermon being broadcast reminded him again that it was Sunday and caused him to grimace. He spun the dial in annoyance looking for a station with country music, then snorted with approval once he had found it. Too much fire and brimstone in these parts, he thought. As if it wasn't hot enough in the desert. Well, the best thing for the heat would be some fire-water. He chuckled at his own pun and looked forward to his first long swig from the flask at his side.

A newscast had come on but he paid no attention until he heard Sam Spencer's name mentioned.

"...was admitted yesterday to Walter Reed Army Hospital with an undiagnosed illness. There has been no word on the Secretary of State's condition and so far hospital officials have refused to comment. The White House has also been strangely silent with the President refusing to comment on whether or not Mr. Spencer's illness would delay the scheduled peace talks. When pressed by reporters as to how soon Mr. Spencer might be able to return to work, Press Secretary Wilson said that he hoped to have more definite information tomorrow..."

Russell Oliver pulled sharply over onto the shoulder of the road. The expression on his face was one of incredulity and shock. John had mentioned trying to call Spencer but no one had seriously entertained the possibility of the Secretary of State falling victim to the disease. With all the turmoil at the hospital, he had completely forgotten about his own promise to call Washington if John's call wasn't returned. It was possible, of course, that he was jumping to conclusions but could it be mere coincidence that Spencer had fallen ill at the same time as John and Bill?

And it was Spencer, after all, who had brought the Indian boy to the hospital in the first place.

The administrator was suddenly seized by a terrible foreboding. He swung the car into a U-turn and pressed the gas pedal to the floor. It was not time for speculation. He knew that he had to return to the hospital immediately and place a call to Washington.

CHAPTER 13 _____

DR. SILVER STARED GLUMLY OUT OF HIS OFFICE
window at a 747 making its ascent from Dulles Airport. In the waning
afternoon hours of that interminable day, the plane symbolized an
escape from the cares that beset him. He found it difficult to believe
that only an hour earlier he had had to conduct the President of the
United States and the head of the Joint Chiefs of Staff to the room of
the Secretary of State. Moments after the President's explosive
outburst on the telephone, Dr. Silver had received a call from the
White House informing him that the President was on his way to
Walter Reed. It was obvious that the President wished to verify for
himself that Sam Spencer was indeed as ill as had been reported.
The visit had been a short one. Dr.Peterson made the introductions
and they immediately went to Spencer's room, where the President
and General Mullins stood at the unconscious Secretary's bedside
and exchanged glances. The only sound in the room was the
electronic beeping of the monitors attached to Spencer's body.

"I want an hourly report on his condition, doctor," said the
President, turning abruptly and walking out of the room. His grim
expression and abrupt manner provoked feelings of guilt in Dr.
Silver. He had been entrusted with the care of one of the country's
most important men and his efforts thus far had resulted in failure.

Closing his eyes, he rested his head against the window pane,
finding the coolness of the glass soothing. He had promised to take
his two grandsons fishing that day and he imagined their
disappointment. A few hurried minutes of conversation with his wife
earlier in the day were all he had been able to manage since the
previous afternoon. Dr. Silver's thoughts had been focused entirely

on Sam Spencer's clinical picture and the lack of response to intensive antibiotic therapy.

'If we're to have any chance at all with Spencer," he had said earlier to Dr. Peterson, "we've got to identify the organism and get sensitivity studies." But there was no way to expedite growth on the culture plates and all he could do was await word from the bacteriology laboratory. If that word was not forthcoming within the next few hours, he knew that it might prove to be academic. The Secretary of State was so gravely ill that it was unlikely at that point that even the appropriate antibiotics would reverse his downhill course.

There was a soft knock on his door and he sighed deeply, grateful for any interruption that would provide a distraction.

"Come in," he called, sitting down heavily in the chair at his desk to await his visitor. He reacted with surprise when Joe Lapides, the hospital's bacteriologist, opened the door. It was apparent from the expression on Lapides's face that he had something to report.

Dr. Silver half rose from his chair and indicated the other chair at his desk. "Sit down, Joe."

"Mark, I think I have something." The five o'clock shadow on the bacteriologist's face and the deep furrows visible on his forehead gave him a debauched appearance but Marcus Silver knew that Lapides had been in the laboratory since Spencer's admission the previous morning.

'Shoot, Joe." He could not understand Lapides's hesitancy in reporting his findings. Ordinarily, the ebullient Greek would have been rattling off his report from the doorway before entering the office.

"We've got some growth on one of the plates—there are gram negative bipolar rods in the sputum."

Dr. Silver responded with a blank look and then raised his eyebrows in confusion. "Gram negative bacilli? Well, what do you suspect, Joe?" he sputtered.

"We're going to begin animal inoculations right away. Guinea pigs and mice. I'm also sending some of the colonies over to CDC in Colorado for them to play with. I know this is going to sound crazy, Mark, but I think we're dealing with plague bacilli."

"Plague bacilli! Oh, shit, Joe, you can do better than that!"

"I can't at the moment. Let's see what happens with the animals. We're also doing sensitivity studies and we're planning further tests on the blood samples we obtained. I hope that by tomorrow we'll know more."

Dr. Silver shook his head in exasperation. "It's not good enough, Joe. Spencer won't hold out that long unless we get on top of this thing. And the way it looks now we're getting nowhere. Plague bacillus! Joe, you know that's ridiculous."

Lapides flushed, bridling at the criticism. "And you should know by now, Mark, that nothing in medicine is ridiculous. I'm not offering explanations, I'm only telling you what we've found."

"I'm not criticizing you, Joe. It's just that we're under tremendous pressure on this. Sam Spencer is no ordinary patient—and it's not every day that I get my ass chewed out by the President of the United States."

Lapides shrugged his shoulders. "I can appreciate your position, Mark, but all we can do is try to come up with the answers. Look, I'm heading back to the lab—I'll keep you posted on every finding. You really ought to get some sleep—you look terrible."

Marcus Silver snorted. "Look who's talking—have you seen yourself in the mirror lately?"

The office door, left ajar by Lapides, opened slightly at that moment and Dr. Peterson peered into the room.

"Come in, Dr. Peterson."

"I'm sorry to interrupt—I didn't know you were busy."

"That's quite all right. This is Joe Lapides, our bacteriologist. Joe, Dr. Peterson."

The two men shook hands as Marcus Silver made the introductions.

"Have you come up with anything on the cultures?" asked Dr. Peterson.

Silver and Lapides exchanged glances.

"Dr. Lapides has identified gram negative bacilli on sputum culture. Identification isn't positive yet but the organism appears to resemble plague bacillus."

Dr.Peterson raised his eyebrows and his mouth opened in astonishment. "But that's not possible," he sputtered, looking from one to the other.

"That was my reaction, too," said Silver. Joe will be doing animal inoculations for verification and we're going to get an opinion from CDC."

"You know, of course," said Peterson, looking at the bacteriologist, "that many other gram negative bacilli could be responsible for Spencer's pneumonitis—coliforms, Klebsiella, Hemophilus—any one of them is a more likely agent than—"

"Dr. Peterson," interrupted Lapides, his face flushed with irritation, "I'm fully aware of that. But I don't choose the organism that grows—and I can only report what is there. With your permission, gentlemen, I should get back to the lab."

"This is preposterous!" exclaimed Peterson when Lapides had left the room. "Surely, Dr. Silver, you know—"

Marcus sighed. "Dr. Peterson, I'm not arguing with you. I'm as perplexed as you are. But Lapides is an excellent bacteriologist—and the thing I find most troubling is that I can't recall one instance when he's been wrong."

Dr. Peterson paced nervously to the window and back, shaking his head. "I just don't understand it." He turned abruptly to face Marcus. "I almost forgot why I had come—I know how busy you are, Dr. Silver, and how involved you've been with this case—and I don't want to intrude, but—this is a bit awkward, I'm afraid."

"What is it you're trying to say?"

The White House physician cleared his throat before continuing. "The President insists that I remain here with you and report to him at hourly intervals on Mr. Spencer's condition."

"He requested the same thing of me. Does the President believe that I can't be trusted to—"

"Please understand, Dr. Silver, it has nothing to do with you. The President is under tremendous pressure right now with the talks coming up and Mr. Spencer's illness has been a serious blow to his hopes for concluding certain agreements that he feels are very important to this country's interests."

"I don't mean to fly off the handle, Dr.Peterson. I suppose that what I find most upsetting is our inability to diagnose and treat this thing. It makes me feel as if I've let the President down."

"That's not true, of course—you've done everything humanly possible—"

"But you know, if Joe Lapides is right, and by some trick of fate

Spencer does have plague, the treatment he's receiving will probably be of no benefit. If memory serves Streptomycin or Tetracycline are the antibiotics of choice. In which case, we've already wasted more than twenty-four hours."

"Oh, really, Dr. Silver, don't you think we should forego this wild speculation and—"

"It may be wild speculation but this infection is not responding to the present treatment and Heaney and Castillo, our communicable disease experts, haven't been able to come up with anything. The other thing is the time factor—it's crucial when dealing with pneumonic plague. If the correct treatment isn't instituted within a few hours after the onset of symptoms, then there's virtually no hope of getting a cure. And given Spencer's present condition, which I'm sure you'll agree is at the point of being hopeless, I don't think we have anything to lose if we treated him as if he did have plague pneumonia. Why don't we go down and see him now. I'm going to change his antibiotic to high doses of Streptomycin and hope that we've acted in time. And don't worry. I'll take full responsibility."

Dr. Peterson followed him from the room, convinced in his own mind that Dr. Silver had lost his reason. He would have to report his opinion to the President when he called but first he wanted to see if there had been any change in Spencer's condition.

They were met at the door of the room by the younger nurse, her excitement apparent. "Dr. Silver, I was just about to put in a call for you. Mr. Spencer appears to be coming out of his coma."

The two men pushed their way past her and found the grey-haired nurse trying to restrain Sam Spencer as he fought to sit up.

Dr. Peterson gave an involuntary gasp at the sight of the struggling figure in the bed. The Secretary of State's cheeks were sunken, almost cadaverous, and his eyes darted feverishly around the room. A pink froth oozed from the corners of his mouth. There was no longer any trace of resemblance between this hideous apparition and the distinguished, handsome figure that adorned the covers of news weeklies with monotonous regularity.

Recovering his composure, Peterson rushed to the bed to help the nurse but Sam had already lapsed into unconsciousness and Peterson assisted the nurse in easing him back down onto the pillow. He noticed that the hospital gown was saturated with perspiration.

"I thought he was starting to come out of it," he said, turning to

Marcus Silver, who was occupied in reading the vital signs record.

Marcus shook his head gravely. "There's been no break in the fever and the pulse rate hasn't dropped. I'm going to call Heaney and Castillo to update them and then I'm going to make the switch to Streptomycin."

Dr. Peterson exhaled deeply, as if resigned to the worst. "I'd better call the President to report," he said, his voice trailing off into a helpless silence.

"You can use the phone at the desk or in my office," said Silver. "Tell the President we're still doing all we can but..."

Sam Spencer remained far removed from the consternation of his two physicians. As Dr. Peterson left the room, the Secretary of State was deeply immersed in a dream that he had had many times before. He stood, a lonely sentinel in the New Mexican desert, surrounded by the awesome saguaros and the mauve peaks of the Sangre de Cristo mountains. His gaze was always to the west for what he awaited would come from that direction. Long hours passed during which the silence was unbroken except for the occasional scurrying of a lizard or the ominous sound of a rattlesnake. High overhead, vultures circled in their anticipation of the desert's offerings.

Dr. Peterson closed the door of Marcus Silver's office and picked up the phone. "This is Dr. Peterson. Please connect me with the White House."

"Oh, Dr. Peterson," said the operator, "I've been trying to locate you. There's a long distance call for you from Mr. Oliver."

"I don't know any Mr. Oliver."

"He says it's urgent, doctor. He's calling from New Mexico."

"All right, put the call through."

Sam's thoughts were directed only to the happiness he had known and to the people he had shared it with. Kate and Jeff. Kate with her flowing auburn hair and hazel eyes. Jeff with his pugnosed, freckle-faced exuberance. He had waited so long for them and now he knew that his waiting would soon be over. They had camped before in this same desert, sitting in quiet harmony around the glow of a campfire, listening to the lonely wails of the coyotes and gazing in rapt admiration at the orgy of shooting stars that transformed the sky into a celestial playground.

"Dr. Peterson, this is Russell Oliver, administrator of the Indian

Medical Center in Gallup, New Mexico. I was shocked to hear about Sam Spencer's illness today."

Peterson made an immediate mental note to chastise the operator for putting through a call of obviously no importance. "Mr. Oliver," he said testily, "I appreciate your expression of concern for Mr. Spencer but I really am quite busy—"

"Doctor, this is damned important or I wouldn't be calling you," shouted Oliver excitedly. "In fact one of my doctors tried to reach Mr. Spencer a couple of days ago and the call was never returned. Did you know that Sam Spencer visited our hospital earlier this week?" Peterson remembered that Spencer had made a short trip to Arizona for a funeral. "I still don't see—" he protested, when Oliver, becoming more impatient, interrupted him.

"Mr. Spencer picked up a sick Navajo boy while driving through Gallup. He brought the boy to us. The boy turned out to have plague pneumonia, Dr. Peterson. Since then we've had a small epidemic here among staff and some of the Indians. It's killed several of our nurses and almost finished off two of our doctors, including the one who tried to reach Spencer to warn him."

Peterson's mind reeled and his voice stuck in his throat. Plague! Lapides had said it looked like plague bacillus.

"Mr. Oliver," he said at last, "are you sure of the diagnosis?"

"Damned sure—we've got positive identification. The goddamn bacillus is deadly, that I can tell you. We've got everyone in the hospital on antibiotics. I'm surprised it didn't make the Washington papers. But never mind that. Do you know what's causing Mr. Spencer's illness?"

"We know he has a pneumonia and—we just grew out gram negative bacilli from his sputum but haven't made a positive identification." Dr. Peterson's voice cracked and faded and his legs felt suddenly weak. He slumped heavily into the chair behind Marcus Silver's desk.

"Oh, God," groaned Oliver.

A silence ensued as each man struggled with his thoughts. The only sound was the long distance hum of the telephone. Dr. Peterson's voice was strained when he spoke again.

"Mr. Oliver, I've got to get back to Mr. Spencer's room at once. I appreciate very much your calling and I'm sure that you'll be hearing from us again." He took down Oliver's number and then walked from

Marcus Silver's office in a state of shock. Lapides had been right and even Silver's hunch had ultimately proven to be correct. Plague! The Secretary of State down with plague in Washington, D.C. It was so absurd, so fantastic, that even now he had difficulty in comprehending it. Suddenly, the word "Boston" flashed across his mind. There had been a case years before in Boston—it had even been reported in the New England Journal. A geologist from Massachusetts had worked in Santa Fe, New Mexico for several days and upon his return to the east coast, had become ill. His condition deteriorated rapidly and he was dead in a couple of days—the cause of death was found to be plague.

Not so absurd after all, he said grimly, unaware that he had spoken the words aloud. Two passing nurses looked at him strangely.

As the grey shroud of night softly enveloped the desert in its folds, headlights suddenly appeared far in the distance near the very spot where the sun had disappeared earlier. Sam felt a joyous anticipation as the lights pierced the crepuscular darkness, coming slowly closer. It was only then that he noticed the strange path the car followed, weaving from side to side, the beams sweeping across the panoply of dunes that surrounded him. A vague fear arose now within his breast and was augmented as the car approached closer, swaying across the desert floor, seemingly out of control of its driver.

At the last moment, when the car was almost upon him, it came to an abrupt stop. The doors flew open and Kate emerged from one side, Jeff from the other. Their faces were not distinct in the deep twilight but he knew it was them. They ran toward him, their arms outstretched and he himself spread his arms wide to enfold them in an embrace of love. The distance that separated them from Sam was negligible, but somehow, in all his previous dreams, although they appeared to be running hard they had never been able to come any closer. This time, however, the distance between them shrank rapidly. No longer able to wait, Sam, too began to run, his heart pounding furiously as he struggled to reach them. "Kate!" he screamed. "Jeff!" I didn't do it! I didn't go along with them!" His agonized cries reverberated from the surrounding hills and suffused the very air of the desert. He could see them more distinctly now as he drew closer and tears streamed from his eyes when he saw they were smiling at him. With a final gasp, he extended his arms until his hands were almost touching Kate's fingertips.

Dr. Peterson pushed open the door to Sam's room. "Dr. Silver," he cried breathlessly, "you were right—I just received a call from—"

"He's gone," said Marcus, drawing the sheet up over Sam's face.

CHAPTER 14 _____

"WELL, DAMN, IT'S GOOD TO HAVE YOU BOTH BACK IN the land of the living!" exclaimed Russell Oliver, effusively greeting John and Bill as they entered his office. Both men had been discharged that morning by Stuart Hollander after having been hospitalized for more than two weeks. The residual effects of the disease were plainly apparent. Each of them had lost about ten pounds and had the sallow, pasty hue of the chronically ill.

"I received word from BIA this morning," said Oliver, "that we can plan on resuming normal operations in a few days so you two couldn't have timed your recovery better." He chuckled. "Yessir, in no time at all you'll both be working your asses off again."

"That will still be better than lying in bed," smiled Bill. "I've been bored stiff."

"Of course, some convalescent time would appear to be in order since you both look terrible. It's a hell of a thing when you can't tell the difference between the doctors and the patients."

"Does the epidemic appear to be over then?" asked John.

"We haven't had a plague case now in two weeks so it looks like we're out of the woods. But the past month was a time none of us will ever forget." He picked up a stack of newspapers from his desk to emphasize his words. "You two were too sick most of the time to appreciate what was going on—and even though you've caught up on all the news it's not the same as following it day by day. It's all here—the most incredible story of our time. And you know," he said, adopting a confidential tone of voice, "we're lucky, too, that heads didn't roll here. Of course, they tried to do a little blame-fixing. Washington asked me why we hadn't alerted the Secretary of State immediately once we had diagnosed plague. I assured them we had tried and gave them the name of that Undersecretary, Dodson, whom you spoke with, John. Well, the son-of-a-bitch must have had to confess that he never followed up on the message to Spencer because a couple of days later I saw in the paper that a certain Undersecretary had 'resigned'. That's a lesson to remember. Cover your ass. Yessir. It's a lesson the Army teaches—and a damned good one."

"What about our friends here in Gallup—Oglethorpe and company?" asked John. "They must be a little unhappy that this whole thing is ending so quickly. They've barely had enough time to feather their nests."

"Ah, the hell with them—and with local politics," grumbled Oliver. Now that the trouble appeared to be coming to an end, Russell Oliver preferred that the animosity that had flared up between himself and Oglethorpe should be forgotten. It was likely that he would soon be able to go back to his golf game and it would be much more pleasant to keep things at an amicable level since they were members of the same country club.

"You know," he said thoughtfully, "I had the strangest feeling when I watched the newsreel footage of Sam Spencer's funeral. It's hard enough to accept the reality of political assassinations, but somehow it was even harder to accept the fact that the Secretary of State contracted pneumonic plague and died, and all because he picked up a sick Indian boy here in Gallup. And then the suspension of the peace talks, the President under medical surveillance, the Walter Reed staff on antibiotic prophylaxis—Jesus, it's unreal.

"Well, anyway, it's all over now—and you fellows are really quite lucky, you know."

"We were in a good hospital," said Bill, winking at John.

"I agree with that, of course," said Oliver, "but we're not Walter Reed—and that's where Spencer was."

"We were lucky enough to have appropriate treatment started within a few hours after the onset of symptoms," said John. "If that Undersecretary had given Sam Spencer the message to call me, if might have turned out differently for him, too. It's too bad. I really liked him."

"Well," said Oliver, "let's all get back to work as quickly as possible. That's the important thing."

John and Bill walked out of the hospital together, acknowledging the smiles and greetings of the well-wishers who gathered around them.

"Ah," said Bill, inhaling deeply as they entered the parking lot, "I never thought we'd see the sun or breathe fresh air again."

John smiled. "You didn't have enough faith," he said, withdrawing Sam Begay's feather-covered rattle from his pocket.

Bill laughed. "I'll just have to start taking some things more seriously. See you back at work." He waved to John as he stepped into his car.

John remained where he was, watching the activity around him. Nothing had changed. Velveteen and calico-clad Navajo women carried their coughing, running-nosed children into the clinic while flannel and denim-clad men in stetsons waited for them by their pickup trucks. He had grown to feel comfortable in this setting and although he would always be an alien in Navajoland, bonds had developed that would forever link him to these people.

Only one thing was missing on this particular summer morning. There was one face he had longed to see when he left the hospital and he was aware of his acute disappointment at its absence. His eyes automatically looked up at Beth's office window but there was no one there. He walked slowly to his car, his legs still rubbery from disuse, and then he saw her. She was standing in front of the old Ford, wearing a flower-print dress and holding a package in her hands. She smiled as he approached and John felt his heart pounding.

They stood facing one another, neither one able to speak. Her lip trembled and John thought she was about to cry. Suddenly she was in his arms and he buried his face in her sweet-smelling hair and kissed her repeatedly. Neither one noticed the smiles of the Indians who watched them. He lifted her chin with his hand and kissed her lips softly.

"I missed you, Beth. I was so afraid for you—"

"Those germs knew better than to mess with me. You'd better be careful," she giggled, as he hugged her tightly. "You'll crush your dinner."

"Is that what's in the bag?" he laughed.

"Well, if you don't let me fix you some good dinners, people are going to mistake you for a skeleton."

"Aren't you working today?"

She shook her head. "It was a holiday and I requested the day off."

"What holiday?"

She touched his cheek with her fingers. "Our holiday."

Beth drove them to his apartment in the Ford. They ascended the one flight of steps slowly with John breathing heavily when they reached the top. "My get up and go got up and went," he gasped.

Beth smiled. "A few weeks in the hospital with a near-fatal illness tends to do that, doctor."

Looking around him as they entered the living room, one of the three large rooms that made up the apartment, John rubbed his finger through the thin layer of dust that had accumulated on the coffee table. "I was beginning to doubt I'd ever see the old place again," he said. "Let's celebrate the raising of Lazarus with some medicinal spirits."

"Tell me where they are and I'll make the drinks," said Beth.

"In the cabinet under the sink. There's scotch and there's vodka, if I remember correctly. I'll have what you have."

Beth brought their drinks and they sat on the sofa, smiling at one another and feeling suddenly shy.

"You know, I was terrified for you," she said.

"It was probably lucky that I was so sick," said John, "or I would have been terrified, too. It's a miserable disease." He gave an involuntary shudder as he thought of the first days of his hospitalization. "I felt so bad when I heard about Sam Spencer's death."

"The whole thing was a nightmare, John."

"I really did like him, Beth. I thought he had a great many things on his mind—not just the pressures of his office, but other things— ghosts would be as good a word as any. And I can understand that. But he seemed to be so guarded against emotion, as if he would be overwhelmed if he permitted himself to feel. But there was something warm and decent underneath—it just didn't have a chance to come out. I hope that he's at peace now."

She nodded. "I wonder if the suspension of the talks might not be for the best. It's difficult to know what was going on behind the scenes but there have been some disturbing reports."

"I guess all we can do is trust in the basic decency of people, national leaders included—and hope that there's even a greater force guiding them.

"Incidentally, Beth, I want to thank you for the gift you gave me." He reached into his pocket and pulled out a small figure. "I know it's a Kachina doll, but what does it represent?"

"It's a Kachina that belonged to my mother's father. It was given to him by a Zuni medicine man and represents Sayatasha, the Rain God. He brings long life."

"It's good to know someone was watching over me. But if it's a family treasure, are you sure you want me to have it?"

"You should know better than to ask."

John withdrew the animal skin rattle from his other pocket. "I got this from Sam Begay, the Singer." He laughed. "Oliver thought my mind had been affected because of this."

Beth's expression turned suddenly serious. "John, I hope you don't think I'm imposing myself on you. I really should have let you be by yourself today and rest."

He reached for her hand. "Beth, you're all I thought about when I was lying in that hospital bed. I felt that the fates had played an unkind trick by bringing you into my life and then separating us the first time we were together. I used to lie there and try to conjure up every detail of your face and try to remember what your laugh sounded like and what your skin and hair smelled like. Please don't stop imposing."

They fell into each other's arms and kissed long and hard. Then, with the early afternoon sun streaming into the room, they undressed and climbed into John's bed. She traced her finger over his now prominent ribs, clucking sympathetically and shaking her head. "Yes, it looks like I'll have to cook quite a few dinners for you."

In the middle of their lovemaking John succumbed to exhaustion and fell asleep in her arms, his head resting on her breast. Beth stroked his back gently and then she, too, fell asleep, a knowing smile on her lips.

EPILOGUE _____

IT WAS ONE OF THOSE BLISTERINGLY HOT SUMMER days on the mesa when even the dry ground cracked in its parched agony. Joseph Williams sat disconsolately in the small circle of shade at the east side of the hogan and stared at the distant horizon, a shimmering indistinct line that melted into the glare of the sun's rays. His grandmother's sheep nibbled at whatever dry brush they could find or sought the poor shade afforded by clumps of ocotillo and cactus.

Joseph and his uncle and grandmother had all been out of the hospital for more than a month, gradually recuperating from their illness. While they were sick, other members of the family had cared for the sheep and helped to raise the money for a Sing for both Mary Begay and Hosteen. Their health restored, they were once more putting in full days of work. Sam Begay had conducted the Windways chant for them upon their discharge from the hospital and now they walked once again in harmony.

Both of them had noticed, however, that Joseph Williams, despite his physical recovery, tended to be moody and kept quietly to himself. At first they wondered if some of the evil spirits still inhabited his body but then Hosteen observed one day, when Joseph was unaware that he was being watched by his uncle, that the boy was tracing something on the ground with a stick.

He walked up quietly behind his nephew and, still unnoticed by the boy, looked down at the figure of a galloping horse. That night Hosteen spoke to his mother about what he had seen and they both knew now that the boy was still grieving for his dead animal.

It would be very difficult to replace the horse. All of their savings had been exhausted by the curing ceremonies and they could not part with any more of their sheep since the flock, too, had been severely depleted during the Sings.

There was only one way now to obtain the cash to buy a new mount for the boy and Mary Begay sighed when she thought of it. She opened a small wooden box stashed in one corner of the hogan. This box had once held all of her jewelry, but the bracelets and rings she had treasured had all been surrendered to the trader as pawn. Only one piece remained—a silver and turquoise squash blossom necklace that had been given to her by her mother. It was a necklace that had no equal for craftsmanship and it was the one piece of jewelry Mary Begay had resolved never to pawn.

She spread it out before her and ran her fingers over the cool patterns of silver and turquoise.

Hosteen watched his mother. He knew what was going on in her mind. "Are you sure you want to?" he asked.

"I am old," she replied, "and a boy needs a horse."

A few days later Hosteen left the hogan very early one morning and reappeared several hours later. He found his sad-faced nephew nibbling on a piece of frybread. Mary Begay looked up from the coffee she was sipping and caught the slight nod of her son's head.

"Come," said Hosteen to Joseph. "There is something I must show you."

Mary remained seated, waiting and listening. She smiled when she heard a squeal of pleasure and a moment later the boy was at her side. His face was transformed and he now looked as happy as she remembered him before his sickness. "Come," he said. "Please come see."

She rose up, cup in hand, and followed her grandson to the door. In front of the hogan stood a magnificent palomino stallion. She watched as the boy walked to the animal and stroked its head, rubbing his cheek against it. Joseph Williams swung his lithe body gently onto the horse's back, careful not to frighten it, and then led the animal into a short canter. Mary Begay turned to look at her eldest son and saw Hosteen's taciturn face break into a smile. It is a good day, she thought to herself as she sipped her coffee.